Tec  e

Hardboiled P.I. Nathaniel Rose:
Bullets, Booze, and Broads

Other books by Michael Bracken

Fiction
- *Deadly Campaign*
- *Even Roses Bleed*
- *In the Town of Memories Dying and Dreams Unborn*
- *Just in Time for Love*
- *Psi Cops*
- *Bad Girls*

Tequila Sunrise

Hardboiled P.I. Nathaniel Rose:
Bullets, Booze, and Broads

Michael Bracken

WILDSIDE PRESS
Berkeley Heights, New Jersey

Copyright © 2000 Michael Bracken.
All rights reserved.

"Partners" first appeared in the Winter/Spring 1988 issue of *Hardboiled*. Copyright 1988 by Michael Bracken.

"Fair Warning" first appeared in *Even Roses Bleed*, published by Books In Motion in 1995. Copyright 1995 by Michael Bracken.

"Heartbreak Hotel" first appeared in *Even Roses Bleed*, published by Books In Motion in 1995. Copyright 1995 by Michael Bracken.

"Lucky Seven" first appeared in *Even Roses Bleed*, published by Books In Motion in 1995. Copyright 1995 by Michael Bracken.

"Even Roses Bleed" first appeared in *Even Roses Bleed*, published by Books In Motion in 1995. Copyright 1995 by Michael Bracken.

"Tequila Sunrise and the Horse" is original to this volume. Copyright 2000 by Michael Bracken.

"Only Business" is original to this volume. Copyright 2000 by Michael Bracken.

Cover art copyright © 2000 by Michelangelo Flores.

Tequila Sunrise
A publication of
Wildside Press
P.O. Box 45
Gillette, NJ 07933-0045
www.wildsidepress.com

FIRST EDITION

to SHARON
with love always

Table of Contents

Partners 9
Fair Warning 19
Heartbreak Hotel 35
Lucky Seven 53
Even Roses Bleed 63
Tequila Sunrise and the Horse 81
Only Business 93

Partners

I stared down the street. Inside the ramshackle white house, just behind the screen, stood the pale blonde I'd awoken next to. I told Lydie good-bye, then I stepped off the porch. As I descended the sagging steps, my shoes nicked off flakes of paint.

I strode across the lawn to my aging Mustang. As I opened the car door, Lydie rushed out of the house, hooked a thin arm around a porch pillar, and leaned over the steps. "Nate," she said. "When will I see you again?"

I turned toward her. "Soon enough," I said. "I'm working on a case."

"This is the big one, right?"

I grunted. In my business there never were any big cases.

I slid into the bucket seat and pulled the door closed. After starting the engine, I released the emergency brake and reached for the stick shift.

Then the Mustang exploded.

Stu Callason sat in the vinyl chair next to my hospital bed and scratched at the five o'clock shadow on his ruddy cheeks.

"You're lucky," he said.

I didn't argue. We'd been a team for three years and I thought I could trust his judgment.

"It was a pro job," Stu said. He would know; he'd toured Vietnam as part of a demolitions crew. "You owe your life to your lady friend. She had you out of the car and halfway across the yard before the gas tank blew."

"How is she?"

"She burned some hair and her left hand's wrapped up pretty good, but she's back home."

"Tell Lydie I'd like to see her."

Stu nodded.

I asked, "Any word from the police?"

He reached a thick hand into the breast pocket of his suit, pulled out a battered notebook, and flipped it open. The pages were covered with a tiny, tight script, using a shorthand only Stu understood. "O'Shannon thinks the dynamite came from a shipment stolen in Des Moines about a year ago. He's got no other clues."

Looking past Stu's broad face and half-lidded eyes, I stared out the window.

"Do me a favor," I said. "Talk to Mannie. Find out who did it and why."

A few days later Lydie visited my room. "I wanted to come sooner," she said, "but Stu said to wait."

She touched at her hair, now cut into a page boy. Her left hand was lightly wrapped. There were no other signs that she'd pulled me from the Mustang.

"I should be out of here soon," I said.

Lydie smiled.

I'd met her almost a year earlier when she'd hired us to do something the police had failed to do: scare away her ex-boyfriend, a dim-witted bruiser with a fondness for beating on women. Stu and I finally convinced the guy that it was in his best interest to avoid Lydie. The alternative was an intimate experience with a steel pipe. She paid our fee with gratitude and a few days later I accepted her dinner invitation.

"How about you?" I asked.

She held up her bandaged hand. "My doctor told me not to sunbathe because I burn too easily. He never warned me away from Mustangs."

I laughed with her, the sound slipping easily from my throat.

When I stopped laughing, Lydie said, "Stu says you've made a lot of enemies over the years. Any of them might want to see you dead." Lydie leaned forward in her chair. "Nobody's talking. Nobody knows anything about it. What can he do?"

"What about Mannie? Has he talked to Mannie yet?" Mannie Goldstein had a finger in just about every pie in town, and if he wasn't in on something, he knew exactly who was.

She shook her head. "Mannie's disappeared."

Two weeks later Stu Callason leaned against the edge of my desk and watched me walk across my office.

"Hell," he said. "The limp ain't so bad."

"The doctor says it should be gone by the end of the year."

"And the burns?"

"A few tender spots. That's all." I walked around my

desk, pulled out my padded leather chair, and sat.

Stu turned to face me, then sat in the chair across the desk from mine. "I closed the Roper file last week," he said. "I found her husband."

"How?" It was the case I'd been working on.

"He used his mother's maiden name, got a phone, and forgot to get an unlisted number. The new phone book just came out." Stu smiled, his thin lips drawn tight across his face.

"Anything else?"

"I'm still working on the Gunderson case," Stu said. Blackmailers took John Gunderson for nearly a quarter of a million dollars, then came back for more. It was a matter too delicate for the police – according to Gunderson – and we'd been called in to solve the problem.

Stu continued, "And we had a guy in here last week wanted us to tail his wife. I told him we were shorthanded."

He reached into his jacket pocket, pulled out a pack of brown cigarettes, and shook one loose. He lit the cigarette, took a few puffs, blew smoke toward the plaster ceiling, then crushed the half-smoked cigarette out in the empty ashtray on the corner of my desk. Finally, his deep-set hazel eyes focused on some spot off to my left, he said, "Look, Nate, I'm working my tail off, but I can't find anybody who knows about the bombing."

I swore under my breath. "Have you talked to Mannie yet?"

"I tried to, but I couldn't get anything out of him. Then he disappeared."

"I'll find him," I said, pushing myself erect. "If anybody knows about this, it's Mannie."

"You better take this." Stu reached under his jacket and pulled a .38 from his shoulder holster. He placed it on my desk.

I looked at the gun and shook my head.

"Have it your way," Stu said. "It's your life."

He seemed relieved when he retrieved the revolver and slipped it back in his holster.

After Stu left, I dialed Lydie's number. I told her I'd be busy all day and suggested we meet at my apartment that evening.

Twenty minutes later I brought a rented Trans Am to a halt in front of Mannie Goldstein's two-story brick house. I quickly made my way to the porch, pounded on the heavy wooden door, waited, then pounded again. When I still received no answer, I reached into the breast pocket of my jacket and pulled out my card. I stuck it in the crack of Mannie's door.

Criss-crossing town, I left a dozen more cards at Mannie's hangouts, always with instructions for him to phone as soon as he turned up. I even left one with Mannie's Rabbi. It seemed a wasted effort; no one had seen Mannie in days.

That night I took a stack of files home. I wanted to see what Stu had done during my absence.

Lydie met me at the apartment door, took me in her arms and kissed me.

"It's good to have you back," she said a moment later.

I stepped away from her, set the files on the coffee table, and peeled off my jacket. Tired and glad to be home, I appreciated Lydie's company.

After seeing Lydie to bed that evening, I went to the living room where I'd left the office files.

As I read through Stu's reports, I discovered everything the way he'd said it was. Most of the cases we'd been working on before I'd gone to the hospital had been solved. A few new cases had been opened. Only the Gunderson case remained unsolved and Stu's reports showed that he'd been diligently working on it.

Gunderson, a wealthy man with business and political connections throughout the city, insisted we avoid contact with the police. Stu's reports showed that he'd done that, but they showed little else. Whoever had the goods on Gunderson was smart. Too smart.

Tired, I rubbed my eyes and closed the folder. It was late and I knew how Lydie liked to start her day.

I went to bed.

When I finally turned up Mannie Goldstein at his brother-in-law's alcoholic rehabilitation center in west county, it took a lot of pressure and fast talking to get past the head nurse. When I finally squeezed into Mannie's room I saw why.

Mannie, a short man with a ring of nappy black hair surrounding the bald crown of his head, had a plump face and sagging jowls. He sported a pair of black eyes. A large, dark bruise marred the side of his fleshy neck. He looked weary and wary.

"What happened to you?"

"Your partner." Mannie's thin, high-pitched voice sounded like he'd never left puberty.

"Why?"

"He asked about the bombing – wanted to know what I'd heard." Mannie backed away from me. The bed caught the backs of his knees and he fell across the mattress, his posterior landing square on the middle of a soiled Burgerbarn Double Barnburger wrapper. "I don't know anything about it."

I towered over Mannie, assessing the damage.

I said, "Sit up."

Mannie sat up.

"You've been straight with me for as long as I've known you."

He nodded, sweat sparkling on the crown of his head.

"You've got to be straight with me now." My voice had a hard, cruel edge I hadn't intended to put there. "Who tried to off me?"

"It was a solo," Mannie whined. "It wasn't a hit. There's no contract on you."

"Did anybody get released from prison recently – anybody I put away?"

"Nobody, Nate. I swear. That's what I've been telling you. There's been talk on the street ever since you got it, but nobody knows anything."

I straightened and Mannie cringed against the wall. When I turned to leave, he said, "Rose? Maybe you should clean your own yard first."

"What's that supposed to mean?" I asked. I stood at the door, not facing him, not wanting to hear what Mannie had to say.

But he didn't say anything else. I left him huddled against the wall and sped across town to my office. When Stu returned from lunch, Agnes sent him straight in.

"I saw Mannie."

Stu dropped into a chair.

"You didn't have to beat on him."

Stu smiled. "I think he enjoyed it."

"He won't be any good the next time I need him."

"Maybe there won't be a next time," Stu said. He picked his nails, not looking at me. "Whoever tried to kill you once will try again."

Stu was right. Somebody wanted me dead. It didn't seem likely they would stop until they succeeded. If it wasn't revenge – and Mannie had confirmed that it wasn't – then it was because I knew something important. I wondered what.

Stu left me alone in the office. He had work to do on the Gunderson case, leads to track that he said would take him all night. I sat at my desk for almost an hour after he left, trying to put together pieces of a puzzle I didn't understand.

After a while I had Agnes bring in the files from past cases. They were alphabetical by year and I'd been in business for nine years. The first year's files took only a few minutes to skim – those had been tough times before Agnes and Stu when I wondered where my next case and my next dollar would come from. Each following year produced increasingly thick stacks.

I read, I considered, I read more. I found nothing. Finally, at seven o'clock, the three-year-old file of the Morton case open on my desk, I gave up. I'd read enough to know Jake Morton had been blackmailed by Peter Coton, a street-smart hood with a long camera lens. Coton still sat in jail.

My head throbbed. I rubbed my temples, found two aspirin in my desk drawer and swallowed them dry, then called my apartment. When Lydie answered, I told her I'd be home soon.

Leaving the files spread across my desk, I switched off the light and left the office.

Lydie surprised me when I arrived home. Naked, she lay across the couch, a glass of red wine in one hand.

Sometime after we'd fallen asleep I heard an unfamiliar sound. I sat up. The light snapped on, blinding me. When I found my focus, I stared at Stu Callason. He pointed a .38 at my chest.

"You son-of-a-bitch," he said.

Lydie rolled over and sat up. The sheet slid to her waist.

"What are you doing here?" I asked. Partner or not, he

didn't belong in my bedroom.

"You remembered the Morton case, didn't you?" Stu said. "I figured you'd be the first to catch the drift. I saw the open file on your desk."

"I was double-checking all the files," I said.

"When did you intended to confront me? In the morning?"

"I wasn't sure about you," I said. I still wasn't. I didn't know what he was talking about.

Lydie sat silently beside me.

"Well I'm sure about you," Stu said. "You'd turn your mother in if you caught her jaywalking. I knew I couldn't trust you. You should be dead already. I certainly did my best."

He straightened his arm. My brain worked double-time. Somewhere inside I matched the blackmail of Gunderson with the blackmail of Morton. Stu linked the two. The Morton case had been his second as my junior partner and he'd wrapped it up so neatly the prosecuting attorney could have slept through the trial and still convicted Coton.

"How many photos did Coton have?" I asked. "Just Morton and Gunderson? Or were there others?"

"Does it matter? Gunderson'll pay whatever I ask or he'll lose everything. The girl was only fourteen."

"How'd you get the photos?" I had to keep Stu talking until I thought of a way out.

"Slid a roll of film into my pocket when the cops weren't looking," Stu said. "Coton picked his targets well. I waited a year but I figured someday the photos might come in handy. Like now. I've a quarter million in a safe deposit box."

I shoved Lydie to the side and rolled out of bed. Stu fired. The bullet tore into the plaster wall behind where I'd been.

I kept rolling. Stu swung the revolver toward me and

fired again. He missed. Lydie threw an alarm clock. It struck his arm. I scrambled to my feet and drove into Stu's midsection with my bare shoulder. We tumbled into the hall.

Stu fired again. Powder burned my arm. Then I knocked the .38 from his fist. It clattered across the hardwood floor. I drove a fist into his face. His nose collapsed.

He pushed me away, scrambled toward the gun. I brought him back down. He rolled under me, then threw me off. I landed on my back. Stu kicked me repeatedly. Pain shot through my abdomen.

I struggled to my feet and he knocked me down again. Stu was tough. He'd always been tough. That's why I'd hired him.

I doubted I could withstand much more.

"Hold it," Lydie said. I couldn't see her, but I knew she stood in the hall with us.

Stu stopped kicking me and stepped away. I looked up. Lydie stood with Stu's .38 grasped in both hands.

He stepped toward her. I couldn't move. Pain tore through my insides.

"Don't," Lydie said.

Stu took another step. Lydie squeezed the trigger. Stu's face exploded. He dropped to the floor and stayed there until the coroner's office hauled him away.

Lydie and I sat together long after the police had finally left. As the sun rose, she held a key before me. "Stu's keyring fell from his pocket. I took this off before the police came."

"A quarter mill," I said quietly. I glanced at my watch. "The bank opens in an hour."

Lydie smiled. "Partners?"

I nodded. For the next few hours we'd fantasize about the money, then I'd drop the key off at O'Shannon's office and stop by the city clerk's office for a marriage license.

Fair Warning

I hit him. Twice.

When Antonio stood, I hit him again. He sat on the barroom floor rubbing his square jaw with one thick hand.

"Mr. D'Angelo doesn't confide in me." He shook his head and grabbed for the edge of the counter to pull himself up.

"Don't move," I said. "I'd hate to hit you again." My hand already throbbed with pain.

Antonio grabbed for my ankle, but he was too slow. I kicked his wrist, then stomped on his hand with the heel of my shoe. He cradled his broken hand in his lap and swore, his voice an octave higher than it had been a moment before. I repeated my question about Bronski.

Antonio looked up at me, his deep-set eyes hidden below a thick brow. "I don't know anything about Bronski."

I knew Antonio lied, but I couldn't make him talk. I dropped a five on the counter for the bartender, then made my way out of the bar and across town to my office.

Agnes was already behind her desk knitting when I entered. Fluorescent light reflected dully from her ebony skin.

"Any calls this morning?" I asked.

"Just one. The bank phoned a few minutes ago."

"Am I overdrawn again?"

"They had a job for you." She glanced nervously down at the desk and rushed ahead. "I turned them down. I told them you don't do repossessions anymore."

I sighed. Repossessions were fast money but they lacked dignity. "You did the right thing, Agnes. If they call again, tell them the same."

Before I stepped through the doorway into my private office, I turned and asked, "How's your granddaughter this morning?"

"She's still the same."

I knew Thelma would never recover, but I always asked.

Closing the door behind me, I grabbed a file folder from the top of my desk, read the phone number typed inside the front flap, and punched it into the desk phone. I was juggling half-a-dozen cases at once and I was glad to be wrapping one up.

A rough male voice answered the first ring. "Monteleone here."

I held the receiver tight against my ear with my shoulder and rifled through the folder. He'd come to the phone faster than I'd expected. "This is Nathaniel Rose, Mr. Monteleone. I've got the information you requested."

"So who's my wife seeing?"

"Your wife isn't seeing just one person," I said as I finally pulled the proper sheet from the folder. "She's seeing a whole group of people."

He swore softly. "I didn't expect that."

"Actually, she's spending her afternoons at a fat farm south of town." I named it for him. "Her doctor says she's lost fifteen pounds since she started. Maybe it's time you stopped being so suspicious of Wilma and started paying some attention to her."

He slammed the phone down.

"Jerk," I said to the dead line. Suspicious husbands had paid many of my bills, but I'd never grown to like them, and I'd liked them even less since Lydie's death.

I stood on the corner on my way to Mrs. Bronski's house to close another case, waiting for the light to change. A black limousine pulled to a halt beside me. Reflective glass prevented me from seeing inside until the rear window on the passenger side snaked down.

"I heard you roughed up one of my boys yesterday," D'Angelo said. He had a ragged voice and a thick Italian accent.

"I gave him fair warning," I replied.

"What is it you wanted from my Antonio?"

"Information."

"You want information, you come to see me. Do you understand that, Mr. Rose?"

"And if I don't –"

"You could be dead the next morning."

"Is that a threat?"

"It's a statement of fact."

"If I need anything," I said through the crack in the window, "I'll let you know."

The light changed before D'Angelo could respond. I crossed the street.

An hour later I sat in Mrs. Bronski's living room. "I'm sorry," I told her. "I'm no closer to finding your husband than I was six months ago."

I reached into the inner breast pocket of my blue pin-stripe jacket and retrieved a thin envelope. I placed it on the coffee table between us.

"I've prepared a final bill," I said. "There's nothing more I can do."

Mrs. Bronski made no move to reach for the envelope. Instead she sat calmly on the overstuffed couch, her long legs tucked under her firm buttocks. She was a buxom brunette just barely my side of thirty – a woman who knew she was attractive, but who didn't flaunt it.

Finally she broke the silence. "Would you care to stay for dinner, Mr. Rose?"

For a brief moment I considered the barren apartment I kept downtown near the office, and all the meals I'd eaten at the Burgerbarn since my wife's death. "I'd be honored."

She stood and ran her fingers through her shoulder-length hair. "Call me Julie, then."

After dinner we sat together on the couch, our knees just barely touching. I had my hands wrapped around a snifter of brandy.

"Do you think he's dead, Nate?"

I was cautious. "He doesn't fit the pattern of a runaway husband."

"You've evading the question."

I took a deep breath. "Your husband's dead. There's no reason to believe otherwise." I thought I knew who'd done it, but not how or why. I didn't tell her that.

Julie was silent for a moment. "Then that's the way it is," she said. "At first I was scared. Then I was angry. Now...now I don't know how I feel."

John Bronski had been gone two months when she'd first called me. The police had officially listed her husband as a missing person and, after a reasonable length of time, had let the case quietly disappear into the files. No remains meant no death; simple, over-worked, under-staffed cop logic. I knew; I'd spent ten years on the force.

Julie gently set her brandy snifter on the coffee table and snuggled under my arm. "Hold me for a minute, Nate."

I held her most of the night.

Burgerbarn, a locally-based chain of fast-food restaurants, had more than two-dozen locations in the metropolitan area. The downtown location was situated midway between my apartment and my office, so I ate most of my meals there.

"You gonna finish that?" O'Shannon said as he squeezed his bulk into the booth a few minutes after I'd arrived. He was pointing at the last half of my Double Barnburger.

"Go ahead." I pushed the styrofoam container across the table to him. Burgerbarn just didn't compare to the meals I'd been getting at Julie's.

"You ever find that Bronski guy?" O'Shannon asked. He spoke with his mouth full of burger.

"Nothing," I told him. "I dropped the case."

"It's just as well." He swallowed and reached for a fistful of my fries. O'Shannon was a good cop, but he had the table manners of a pig. "Anyhow, I've been looking through my files for you. I haven't got much."

I took a swallow from my Pepsi, then offered the remains to O'Shannon. "Anything you've got is fine."

"A lot of bad shit's been hitting the street lately, right? Well, we can't pin any of it on the D'Angelo family. They're running it through a front and laundering the money somehow."

"But you're sure it's D'Angelo?"

"Give me a break, Nate. Who else could it be?"

The D'Angelo family had the city by the nose. The elder D'Angelo had grown up fast and street smart in the 1930s when his father controlled the city. They'd started with prohibition booze and moved up to hard drugs. The family restaurant, now respectable, had begun as a gin joint.

"Who's your client on this one?" O'Shannon asked.

"Agnes' granddaughter got some bad coke. She's in a

coma."

O'Shannon sat silently. "Look," he finally said, "I wish I could help but we don't have anything on him."

After I left O'Shannon, I visited a small pawn shop a dozen blocks away. I knew I could trust Freddie the Fence; I'd dealt with him many times. For the right amount of money Freddie could locate anything that had been fenced during the previous year. And he could usually retrieve it.

The ferret-faced little black man was leaning against the counter when I entered the shop.

"I need a favor from you, Freddie."

He eyed me carefully and listened while I explained the situation.

"I don't mess with drugs," he said when I finished. "You know that."

"All I want is a name, Freddie."

"You say it's a sister?"

I nodded.

"I'll see what I can do."

Julie was waiting for me when I returned to the office.

"Coffee?" I asked.

"No, thanks."

I poured myself a cup, then leaned on the edge of my desk. My three-room, second floor office wasn't in the most prestigious building, but I'd gone out of my way to be sure no one could tell from the inside. The furnishings were fashionable and comfortable. I motioned Julie into a seat.

"I have a new case for you, Nate," she said. She'd already paid for the abortive search for her husband. She was a good client – she paid well and she kept my thoughts from dwelling on Lydie – but I was having difficulty defining the difference between client and confidant.

"My husband's lawyer called me today. He received a sizable offer for my portion of the Burgerbarn chain. I want to know who made the offer."

"He didn't tell you?"

"He didn't say and I don't trust him. My husband hired his firm."

"How much do you hold?"

"Twenty-five percent. Fifty-two percent is owned by a holding company. The rest is spread between a few dozen smaller stockholders."

"Did he tell you anything else?"

"Only that John had refused an offer for the same stock shortly before his disappearance."

Agnes poked her head through the open doorway. "Mr. Rose? Victor Monteleone just phoned. He said he received your bill this afternoon."

I took a sip from my coffee mug.

"He said you could stuff it."

Julie left a few minutes later – after I'd accepted the new case and an invitation to dinner. Then Freddie the Fence called. I noted his information and made an appointment to see O'Shannon.

When I walked into his mid-town office an hour later, O'Shannon was biting off half a Milky Way. "You want some?" he asked.

I shook my head. "There's an airstrip across the river where the cocaine comes in."

"We don't have jurisdiction over there." O'Shannon swallowed and took the other half of the candy bar into his mouth.

"You don't need it." I explained exactly where and how it crossed the river into St. Louis. "I just don't know when."

O'Shannon sat upright and reached for his notebook. "Give me what you've got and I'll pass it along to narcotics."

"No names attached," I said. When O'Shannon agreed, I told him what Freddie had told me.

"Look," I said into the phone, "It's a simple request. I want to know who holds the controlling interest."

"Another holding company."

I swore silently at my broker. "And who controls that?"

"It's a complex trail, Nate. I've been at it all afternoon."

"Just give me the bottom line."

I heard papers shuffle. "Ultimately," he said, "it's controlled by a trust fund administered by a pair of Polish lawyers." He gave me their names. One of them was the lawyer Julie had inherited from her husband. The trust fund had been set up for a group of children, but I didn't recognize their names.

When I hung up the phone, Agnes stepped into my office. She stood reluctantly before my desk.

"Something up?" I asked.

"If I could get off a little early, I'd like to see Thelma. Joey phoned from the hospital and said she's getting worse."

I glanced at my watch. It was half past three. "Call a cab," I said. I reached into my pocket and handed her a twenty. I didn't want her taking the cross-town bus.

After Agnes left, I settled into the chair behind my desk and started reading a paperback mystery. I wanted to relax before dinner with Julie. I was just finishing the first chapter when a sound in the outer office caught my attention.

"Hello?" I said as I opened the door to the reception room. Antonio grabbed my collar and slammed me against the wall. Then he back-handed me with the cast on his right hand. His carbon-copy grabbed my arms and held me upright.

"Mr. D'Angelo said you've been asking too many questions. He sent me to give you a message." Antonio hit me again. When I struggled, Antonio's ebony helper tightened his grip on my arms.

After the first blow to my face, Antonio was careful to strike only my mid-section. Before long I vomited on my Brooks Brothers pin-stripe and splattered my lunch across the two attackers. They dropped me to the floor.

"And one more thing," Antonio said. "If you don't get your nose out of Mr. D'Angelo's business, he's going to put you through the grinder like he did Mr. Bronski."

I was barely conscious. I mumbled, "What'd he do to Bronski?"

Antonio laughed. "He was the main course at Burgerbarn. We made hamburger out of him."

I realized how often I'd eaten at Burgerbarn and vomited again.

They left me crumpled against the wall of my office.

I was an hour late when I arrived at Julie's front door. She was upset, but then she saw the bruise on the side of my head.

"What happened?"

"Some unfriendly people," I told her.

Julie ushered me into the house and sat me on the couch. I'd managed to wipe off my suit, but the dark stain on my jacket remained. I hadn't stopped at my apartment to change.

Julie rushed into the bathroom and returned with a warm, damp washcloth.

"I'm afraid dinner's ruined," she said. Then she carefully brushed back my damp hair and washed off my forehead. She loosened my tie and unthreaded it from my shirt collar, unbuttoned the top few buttons of my shirt and helped me pull off the vomit-soaked jacket and vest. After I'd begun to relax, she handed me a snifter of brandy.

Antonio and his friend hadn't damaged anything of value. I had a few bruises and I had a dull, throbbing pain running through most of my body, but no bones were broken and it didn't feel as if any internal organs had been damaged. It had been a warning shot, nothing more.

And it had been a fair warning. D'Angelo wanted me to drop a case, but now I didn't know which one.

"Why'd they do it?" Julie asked. She slipped off her high-heels and laid them on the thick shag carpet.

"I'm too close to something," I told her. "But I can't put the pieces together yet."

Julie knelt on the floor beside me. "Worry about it tomorrow," she said.

She eased me back against the end cushion and slowly finished unbuttoning my shirt. I took her face in my hands and pulled it close to mine. I kissed her, my lips trailing away across her cheek and down her neck to the collar of her pale blue blouse.

Something about Julie made me forget Lydie.

Julie had the morning paper on the night stand for me when I woke. I rubbed my eyes with my knuckles and spotted the headline. During the night 23 people had been arrested for possession of narcotics with intent to sell. Across the river, two Illinois narcs had confiscated a private plane and arrested its pilot and two-member crew.

Freddie the Fence had been right and O'Shannon's fellow officers had put all the pieces together perfectly. D'Angelo had been indirectly implicated by two of the ar-rested men and a related article described D'Angelo's alleged criminal activities and mentioned his three daughters by their married names.

I dropped the newspaper on the night stand, threw back the covers and pushed myself out of bed. My body still ached. I called Julie's name, then followed the sound of her answering voice to the living room. I sat facing her.

"I have to tell you this," I said, "but I don't want to." The newspaper had put all the names together for me and I began explaining the situation to her.

"I don't think your husband realized it, but his lawyer is co-administrator of a trust fund for the D'Angelo grandchildren. The family has been using the Burgerbarn chain to launder some of their drug money. Although it's sold over-the-counter, most of the stockholders are members of the D'Angelo family, or they work for D'Angelo. Your husband was the biggest stockholder who wasn't a family member. They made a legitimate offer for his stock. When he refused to sell, they processed him through the grinders."

Julie blanched.

"Now they've made you an offer for the same stock. My advice is to sell it. Then find yourself a new lawyer. D'Angelo's got yours in his hip pocket."

I glanced at my watch. It was after nine. "Call your lawyer now and approve the transaction. Your life could depend on it."

Julie reached for the phone, flipped through a list of phone numbers with the other hand, then dialed. I listened for a moment.

"Mr. Stanovski please...this is Mrs. Bronski...yes, I'll hold." She cupped her hand over the phone and looked at me. I stood and headed for the bathroom. I was sure she understood what to do.

Two hours later I pulled to a halt in front of Freddie's pawn shop. The area was cordoned off and police swarmed the neighborhood. I stepped from my car and watched.

O'Shannon caught my eye and waved me over. "What are you doing here, Nate?"

"I came to see Freddie."

"It's too late. Somebody gave him the final good-bye." O'Shannon dug in his pocket for a bag of M&Ms. "Six shots. He's spread all over the back wall." O'Shannon shook his head. "Didn't stand a chance."

"Who did it?"

"No witnesses," he said. "But the style is familiar. Freddie must have made D'Angelo awfully angry. It's been a long time since he wasted anybody like this."

I hadn't told O'Shannon where I'd gotten the info on the drug shipment, but D'Angelo had figured it out.

I left O'Shannon to his work and went to my office. It was empty when I arrived at eleven. I reached for the phone and dialed Agnes' home number.

Her husband answered, recognized my voice, and said, "She's at the parlor with Joey. Thelma died last night. She never came out of the coma."

I told him to let Agnes know she could have the week off with pay, then I hung up. I walked into my office, reached into the bottom drawer of my desk, and pulled out an unregistered .45 and a shoulder holster. I'd grown familiar with the pistol during a brief tour of Korea, but I'd avoided wearing it on the job because of Lydie.

From another drawer I pulled two full clips for the pistol. I slid one into place and dropped the second into my jacket pocket. I strapped on the shoulder holster and retrieved my jacket.

On the way to Julie's, I stopped at a travel agency for a one-way ticket to Honolulu.

When Julie answered my pounding at her front door I grabbed her tightly, then stuffed the ticket in her hand. "There's something going down and I don't know if it involves you or not."

She looked at the ticket. "Honolulu?"

"You've got to get out of town. Come back in a few weeks. I'll let you know when it's safe." I took a quick breath. "Have you got a suitcase?"

"In the closet."

"Get it out and get it packed. The plane leaves in two hours."

Julie pulled the suitcase from the closet, carried it into her bedroom, and dumped in on the bed. I helped her stuff it with warm-weather clothing, then carried it out to her car.

"I forgot the ticket," she said. She was standing beside the car.

"Where?"

"On the bedroom dresser."

She opened the car door and dropped into the seat as I headed up the walk to the house. As I stepped through the front door, the car exploded. The force sent me sprawling across the foyer.

When I rolled over and looked through the open door Julie's car was a mass of flames. She was dead. There was nothing I could do for her. I phoned the fire department. Then I called O'Shannon.

"What'd they want to kill her for, Nate? What's happening?"

I hung up.

Outside, past the smoldering hunk of metal where Julie's body had disintegrated, I climbed into my car. Tears pooled at the corners of my eyes. Perhaps I'd loved Julie, perhaps she'd just helped me ease the pain of my wife's slow death. It didn't matter what I'd felt for Julie because now even she had been taken from me.

I drove. And I thought. At first I didn't pay attention to where I headed. Then, when I realized I was in a familiar neighborhood, I located a house I'd watched for nearly a month, pulled the car to the curb, and headed up the walk.

I pounded on the front door. A moment later Victor Monteleone pulled the door open. "What the hell are you doing here?"

"I've come to collect." I pushed the door open and stepped past him into the living room. His wife stared at me from the couch.

"I don't owe you anything," he said.

"Do I tell Wilma who I am?"

Monteleone stared at me for a moment, then said, "I'll get my checkbook."

I followed him to the kitchen. "Save your money." I shoved a piece of paper in his hand. "Call this number. Ask for Mr. D'Angelo. Tell him you have a message from Mr. Rose. Tell him this is a fair warning."

Monteleone looked at the number, then at me.

"We'll call it even," I said.

Monteleone reached for the wall phone and punched in the numbers. I stood next to him as he delivered the message.

Then he said, "Who am I? I'm Victor Mon –"

I disconnected the line with my forefinger, then took the slip of paper with D'Angelo's number on it from Monteleone's hand. "We're even," I said.

I walked back through the house and opened the front door. As I pulled it closed behind me, I heard Wilma ask, "What was that all about?"

At a phone booth a mile away, I dialed O'Shannon's number.

"Nate? Where the hell have you been?"

"Meet me in twenty minutes," I said. "No sirens." I gave him an address, then I hung up on his next question. I climbed into my car and headed east, toward the south side where the D'Angelo family restaurant had served the city since the thirties.

Twenty-two minutes later I pulled my car to a halt and

stepped into the shadows of the restaurant. The last place D'Angelo expected me was on his home turf. His boys had been scoring people all around me. My people. I knew I would soon come to the top of his list.

I drew the .45 from my shoulder holster and turned the safety off. Holding the gun close to my side, I walked around to the front of the restaurant. O'Shannon sat in an unmarked car across the street. I ignored him.

I raised the pistol and stepped into the dimly lit restaurant. D'Angelo and two of his boys sat at a table in the rear.

"D'Angelo," I yelled.

He turned. Antonio jumped to his feet and pulled a revolver from his waistband. His ebony assistant stood.

I squeezed off the first shot. Antonio spun around and crashed across the next table. Blood seeped from his chest.

The second shot splattered D'Angelo's brains across the back wall.

The door crashed open behind me. The remaining man at D'Angelo's table – the black man who'd held me while Antonio had rearranged my insides – drew a revolver and fired back. I heard O'Shannon swear beside me, but I didn't look away until the seventh empty shell from my .45 clinked to the floor and everyone at D'Angelo's table was dead.

I slumped into an empty seat.

O'Shannon stood over me. "This'll be a bitch to explain."

I looked up at him. I waved the empty .45 at the bodies. "They owed me something," I said. They owed me something I could never regain.

O'Shannon walked across the restaurant, wrapped a handkerchief around his hand, and drew a revolver from under D'Angelo's coat. He fired two shots in my direction, then placed the gun in D'Angelo's hand.

He walked back, sat across the table from me, and pulled out a Milky Way. "Looks like self-defense," he said as he unwrapped the candy bar. "It's a good thing I happened to be in the neighborhood."

Heartbreak Hotel

A thick-shouldered lummox in a grease-stained blue workshirt sat at the end of the bar nursing a mug of beer. He silently watched while I questioned the bartender.

The bartender, a slender man with a pencil-thin mustache waxed to a point at each end and black hair greased straight back from his forehead to his shirt collar, shook his head negatively after each question. "I'm sorry," he said. "I don't know anything about it."

Charlie Fischer had been an occasional source of information over the years, so I dropped a five on the counter of his dark near-north side bar.

As I was leaving, the lummox in the workshirt hauled himself to his feet and stood between me and the door. "You looking for trouble?" he asked in a voice thick with the gravel that comes from years of heavy smoking.

"Actually," I said, "I'm looking for Andrea Stewart."

"Well you found trouble." He swung a meaty fist toward my face. I neatly side-stepped the blow.

He swung a second time and again I side-stepped his fist. The lummox was too drunk to take careful aim and I continued ducking his blows while Charlie edged his way down the length of the bar, a blackjack in his hand. Turning as I slowly circled him, the lummox soon had his back to the bar. Charlie braced himself with one hand on the worn wood, reached quickly across the top of the bar, and tapped my assailant on the top of his head.

The lummox staggered, then collapsed between two bar stools.

"That's why I don't stop by very often," I told Charlie. "You attract a rough clientele."

Charlie returned the blackjack to its hiding place under the bar, then walked around to my side to look down at the unconscious man.

"Who is he?" I asked as I patted his pockets, searching for a wallet.

"Beats me," Charlie said, shrugging his shoulders. "He's been coming in off-and-on for the past year but nobody seems to know much about him. He's been pretty quiet until now."

I found the lummox's wallet and flipped it open to the driver's license. I read the name to Charlie. "Max Drummond. Mean anything to you?"

Charlie shrugged again. "Nothing."

I continued thumbing through Drummond's wallet, stopping when I came to a blurry photo of the lummox with his arms around a petite brunette. I reached into the breast pocket of my suit and pulled out another photo. I squinted at them in the darkness of the bar, then said, "Is this the same woman, Charlie?"

He looked at the photos, then walked around the bar to the light switch. Fluorescent light flooded a small section of the bar and Charlie returned to study the photos.

What I'd pulled from my suit pocket was a corporate identification photo of a young woman in her mid-twenties, with long brown hair flowing down to her softly-rounded shoulders. Her hazel eyes stared at some point off to the right of the camera.

"Can't tell, Nate, but she looks similar," Charlie finally said.

"Okay," I told him. "Let's wake up our friend."

Charlie filled a dirty beer mug with cold tap water and slid it across the bar to me. I splashed water onto Drummond's face and watched him sputter as he pulled himself to his feet. He dropped onto a bar stool and brushed back his short black hair with his meaty fists.

When he realized I had his wallet open on the bar before me, Drummond angrily said, "Where'd you get that?"

"Your pocket," I said. "You weren't using it."

"Give it back." He held out a hand.

"Tell me about Andrea first," I said. I slid the wallet a few inches toward Drummond, but kept it out of his reach.

"Who are you?"

Charlie reached under the bar for his blackjack and rested it on top of the bar next to his hand. He listened attentively.

"Let's just say I'm an interested party," I said.

Drummond looked at Charlie's blackjack, then he looked at me. "She was my fiancee."

I studied Drummond for a moment. He was big and powerful, but he was packing too many excess pounds on his frame. His blue workshirt was stretched tight across his abdomen and his jowls flapped loosely as he spoke. I said, "You don't look like her type."

His eyelids narrowed. "How well did you know her?"

"Never met." Although I occasionally did some security work for the electronics firm where she was employed, I'd never heard of Andrea Stewart until her case crossed my desk. She'd spent the last three years working as a clerk for the firm and four days after she disappeared, her temporary replacement couldn't find a series of files dealing with some government contract work the firm had been doing. That's when the case had been jobbed out to me. Security had been breached and I'd been hired to plug the leak before the feds learned about it.

Drummond shrugged, then rubbed at the knot on the back of his head. "Could I get a another beer?"

Charlie took the blackjack with him as he moved down the bar to fill Drummond's request.

"Where is she now?" I asked.

"How the hell should I know?" Drummond turned back toward me. "I haven't seen her for two weeks." He took the mug from Charlie's outstretched hand and swallowed a quick gulp of beer. "She's disappeared. No note, no letter, no phone call. I went to her room one night after work and she was gone."

I waited, sensing that Drummond had more he wanted to say.

"I know I'm not the prize catch," he continued after another swallow of beer, "and she didn't have to marry me if she didn't want to. But, damn it, she could have had the courtesy to say good-bye."

I waited while Drummond fought back a quiver in his voice, then I asked, "Where was she living?"

Drummond pointed toward the back wall of the bar. "Around the corner at the Heartbreak."

I stood. "You can put that away," I said to Charlie Fischer as I pointed at the blackjack. "I don't think he'll cause any more trouble."

Drummond looked up at me when I slid his wallet down the bar to him. "When you find her," he said, "you tell her I want to see her."

I replaced the company photo of Andrea Stewart in my breast pocket.

"You'll do that, won't you?" he pleaded. "You'll tell her, won't you?"

"I'll tell her," I said. Then I left.

Outside the bar I turned right, then turned right again

at the corner. The broiling mid-afternoon sun beat down on the back of my neck and I began to sweat. My armpits were cesspools of perspiration by the time I strode through the doors of the hotel – a women-only establishment nicknamed the Heartbreak Hotel by the dozens of men whose romances had been shattered by the hotel's residents.

I approached the wiry old man behind the counter, tossed Andrea's photo in front of him, and asked, "Do you know her?"

The desk clerk's eyes narrowed to suspicious slits; the wrinkles in his face tightened. "What if I do?"

"Just answer the question," I told him. "There's no reason to get hostile."

"So who are you?" He stood defiantly behind the counter.

"Nathaniel Rose," I said. "I'm an investigator."

"Show me your badge."

"I'm private," I said. I usually worked nickel-and-dime cases – even stooping to repossessions and divorce cases when times were tough – but a former colleague had taken his police pension and gone to work for the electronics firm. Every so often they had a case that involved actual investigation and that's when he jobbed the work out to me. It was a sweet deal for both of us – I got double my usual fee and he didn't have to wear out any of the leather on his Italian loafers. It was a sweet deal, that is, until I met up with guys like this hotel clerk.

"Get the hell out of my hotel," the little man screamed. A dozen female faces turned to stare at us.

I picked up the photo. Loudly, I asked, "Was Andrea Stewart living here?"

"I said out!" He pulled a revolver from behind the counter. "I don't want your kind snooping around. Respectable women live here."

I swore under my breath as I looked up the revolver's

barrel from the wrong end. Backing away from the little man, I raised my hands in supplication.

Once outside, I stood and stared at the eight-story building. Although run-down like the rest of the neighborhood, the Heartbreak Hotel wasn't the end of the line for most of its residents. Within ten blocks stood most of St. Louis's new glass-and-steel office buildings, home offices for half-a-dozen Fortune 500 companies, a handful of major banks, and the electronic firm's main paperwork center.

The hotel's residents all worked within walking distance of the Heartbreak, their collective fingers all poised on the pulse of the midwest.

When I turned to walk back to my car, I heard hurried footsteps approaching me from behind. Before I could turn around again, a buxom blonde in a yellow silk blouse and a pleated knee-length skirt caught my elbow and whispered, "Keep walking."

I did. When we reached the corner, she said, "I heard you asking about Andrea. She lived across the hall from me." She caught her breath as she slowed our pace. "Can we talk?"

I guided her into the Pink Flamingo, noted with satisfaction that Max Drummond had already vacated the bar, and ushered her into a booth at the far end of the room. Charlie approached to take our drink order but I waved him away before he could interrupt us.

"Do you have a name?" I asked.

"Sandra Dennison," she said, her voice soft as velvet.

I told her my name.

"Why were you looking for Andrea?"

"Her uncle died and left her some money," I lied. "The only thing the lawyer knew when he called me was that Andrea was living on the near-north side and that she didn't have a phone number listed in her name." I paused for a breath and studied the softness of Sandra's oval face, her full lips delicately parted as she listened to me, her pale blue eyes wary and alert. I continued. "It took me almost three days to trace her to the Heartbreak."

"How much is the lawyer paying you to look for Andrea?"

I said, "Enough." Then I asked, "Where is she?"

Sandra shook her head, her platinum blonde curls swinging freely. "She left two weeks ago. I don't know where she went."

"Why'd she leave?"

"Don't know."

Through the corner of my eye I could see Charlie leaning over the end of the bar, straining to hear what we were saying.

"She was always quiet," Sandra said. "Andrea never bothered anybody. It was quite a surprise when she disappeared."

"Why didn't somebody report it to the police?" I asked.

Sandra answered my question with a question. "Why? Her rent was paid up and she didn't have to report to anybody. If she wants to leave without telling us, that's her business."

"Did you suspect something was wrong after two weeks?"

Sandra laughed. It sounded forced. "Other girls have been gone longer. They were all just fine when they returned."

"What about her fiance?"

Sandra eyed me forcefully.

"Wouldn't she have told him?"

"He was an ass. I don't think Andrea loved him."

"He seems to love her."

"That's too bad," Sandra said. She took a deep breath. "That's just too bad."

Further questioning led nowhere, even though Sandra had approached me. Intending to ask more questions, I invited Sandra to dinner the following evening. Sandra glanced nervously toward Charlie, then agreed.

After she left, I walked up to the bar, hoisted myself onto a stool, and ordered my first drink of the day. When Charlie placed the Irish Whiskey before me, I took a huge swallow of the drink and swore at myself.

The next day I found Max Drummond underneath a battered red Peterbilt, his hands covered with grease. He wiped them on the front of his workshirt, then stuck one grimy paw toward me and said, "Look, I'm sorry about yesterday. I made a fool of myself."

I took his hand in mine, shook it solidly, accepting his apology. When Drummond released his grip on my hand, I said, "What do you think happened to Andrea?"

"I don't know. I don't think she would just walk out like that, not two months before our wedding," he said. "Not the Andrea I knew."

"Someone told me that Andrea didn't love you," I said. "They intimated that she may have wanted to break off the engagement."

"Who said that? One of those broads at the hotel?" I could see the anger rising in Drummond's face. He continued. "They didn't like me. None of them did. They didn't want me to see Andrea."

"But you kept seeing her –"

"Damn right. I saw her every day up until she disappeared."

"What day was that?"

"July 31st. I remember it like it was yesterday. I kissed her good-bye at the hotel's south doors. She said she had something important to do that night, something that was going to be a big surprise, and then she hurried inside. The next day I went to the hotel and they said she was gone."

"*Who* said she was gone?"

"The little bastard at the desk," Drummond said. "I

made him take me up to her room and prove it. I'd never been up there before. I couldn't tell if any of her things were gone, but I knew she wasn't there. They must have done something to her because I haven't heard from her since."

"What are you going to do now?" I asked.

"I don't know. I just don't know." He paused as if thinking something over. "Look, I don't know who hired you to find Andrea, or why, but if you find her I'll give you everything I've got. It's only a few thousand, but it's yours."

"No thanks," I said. "I don't need another client on this case." I pulled an embossed business card from my pocket and shoved it into his fist. "You call me if you think of anything that might help. If I'm not there, tell your story to Agnes."

"I will," he said. "You can bet on it."

I left while he studied the face of the card.

My next stop was the Heartbreak Hotel. Instead of entering the lobby to become a moving target for the scrawny idiot behind the desk, I studied the hotel from the outside, counting doors and windows, mentally measuring the distance from one to the other. I slowly walked all the way around the hotel, picking my way through the garbage in the alley behind the building.

Just before the alley opened onto the hotel's parking lot, I found an untended door. I easily picked the lock and slipped into the back of the hotel unnoticed. Quietly, I walked down the corridor, opening each door I came to until I found the basement. I slipped through the door and followed the dark steps until I felt my patent leather shoes strike concrete.

The elevator motor thrummed quietly in the darkness. I waited until I was positive I was alone, then I snapped on a light and peered at the broken furniture surrounding me. I carefully moved through the chairs, sofas and beds, noting how clean everything was. Once past the furniture, I eased around a solid-looking set of shelves and found myself on the edge of a large, empty area. On the other side of the basement, near the elevator equipment, was a door. I went to the door, opened it, and looked up a brightly lit stairwell. I didn't know Andrea's room number so I abandoned any thought I had of climbing the stairs.

I turned around again, letting the door close quietly behind me. I recrossed the open area, stopping at the shelves. The first few were filled with paint cans and brushes, the next with tiny plastic boxes filled with screws and nails, the last few with an assortment of carpenter's tools. The basement told me nothing about Andrea; it told me a lot about the Heartbreak.

Touching nothing, I made my way around the shelves and back through the furniture to the rear stairs. I snapped off the light, eased my way up the stairs, and stepped out into the rear corridor. I tried to follow the corridor deeper into the hotel, but found my way blocked when it made a sharp turn and opened up onto the lobby. I flattened against the wall, scanned the lobby carefully, noting the position of all the furniture in relationship to the doors.

Satisfied with my reconnaissance, I returned to my car and drove to my office. I spent the rest of the day sorting through the paperwork involved with Andrea Stewart, reading and rereading everything in her personnel file until I'd gone through six cups of Agnes' coffee and two trips to the john.

There wasn't much to work with. Andrea Stewart had left Boston three years earlier and made her way halfway across the country to St. Louis. Her initial interview had gone well, her background had been clean – except for a failing grade in a college biology course – and she'd been hired almost immediately. She'd proven herself trustworthy over the years and had been moved up accordingly. At the firm a move up meant increased access to sensitive material.

Andrea's photo had been in the file when I'd first received it from the electronics firm and Agnes had made copies for me. When I'd visited the address in Andrea's personnel file, I'd found a burned-out shell of a building and no forwarding address. When I'd tried the phone number in her file I discovered the phone had been disconnected.

Someone in personnel hadn't kept Andrea's records up-to-date and I had reported it to the appropriate vice president. Then I'd started my search.

I threw the file on the desk in disgust. Andrea Stewart was an enigma, one that was becoming increasingly frustrating to search for. The mental picture I kept getting was that of a wide-eyed innocent, yet she had picked Max Drummond to be her future husband and had somehow become involved with Sandra Dennison.

Disgusted with myself for failing to follow the trail Andrea must have left behind, I returned to my apartment to prepare for my dinner date with Sandra. I met her outside the Heartbreak Hotel and drove her to a quiet restaurant near Forest Park.

Dinner went smoothly enough, but every time I tried to bring up Andrea's name, Sandra avoided my questions. Mostly what she did was flirt with me, licking her upper lip with just the tip of her tongue, lightly rubbing her legs against mine under the table, and turning her torso just enough so that the front of her low-cut blouse bulged open.

Over dessert, she said, "You know, Nathaniel, I find you *very* attractive."

I'd mixed business with pleasure many times before and I knew a come-on when I heard one. I let her know the feeling was mutual.

"Maybe we could stop by your place after dinner," she suggested, her voice husky with the hint of sex.

Safely in my apartment half-an-hour later, I prepared drinks for us and carried them into the living room. "How well did you know Andrea?" I asked as I handed Sandra her drink.

"As well as any neighbor, I suppose." She took a tentative sip from the glass, then set it aside.

"How long did Andrea live in the –"

"Let's not talk about her now." Sandra stood and pressed herself against me. Her body was firm, her embrace was strong.

"Did she –"

Sandra pressed her full red lips against mine, silencing me. I felt her tongue force its way into my mouth and I tasted the sweetness of her. Before long, thoughts of Andrea disappeared.

After Sandra left that night, I pulled on a robe, took a light beer out of the refrigerator, and settled into my favorite chair to stare at the television. Instead of watching the boring sitcom that flickered across the television screen, my mind worked overtime.

Something about Sandra Dennison bothered me and I wasn't sure what it was. Maybe it was the way she avoided my questions – simple questions about Andrea Stewart. If Sandra hadn't wanted to talk to me, she shouldn't have agreed to dinner. She wanted something from me but refused to give me anything in return. I didn't like that. I didn't like that at all.

I pushed myself out of the easy chair and went to the phone. I dialed Max Drummond's number, waited until he answered on the fourth ring, and asked him for Andrea's room number.

Then I dressed, went to my office, and collected my .45 and my shoulder holster. As I strapped it on, I remembered all the times Lydie had insisted I leave it in the office, and all the times I'd come back for it while working one case or another.

A few minutes later I brought my aging Chevy to a halt near the Heartbreak. I left the car and quickly made my way to the alley. After picking the lock on the untended rear door, I slipped quietly down the corridor to the basement door, and stepped through it. I let my eyes adjust to the darkness, then I slipped through the old furniture, across the basement to the other doorway. Five flights up the other stairs, on the fourth floor, I stepped into the hallway. The thick, dark blue carpet muffled my steps as I made my way down the hall to room 4B. Seconds later I was inside Andrea's room. I closed the door behind me, waited a moment in silence, then snapped on the light. From the street, Andrea's room light could be seen. I hoped it wouldn't matter.

Andrea had one large room and a bath. A neatly-made double bed had been tucked into the far corner, a three-drawer dresser beside to it. Travel brochures nearly covered a small desk behind the door and the particle board bookcase next to it held a smattering of classics and paperback romances. Along the wall to the right was a sink, a range, and a half-size refrigerator. A white formica table with four chairs surrounding it sat off-center in the room, nearer the sink than anything else. Dust covered everything like a cheap blanket and the fern on the table needed watering.

I examined the travel brochures, searched through the desk and the bookcase, then pulled open one of the dresser drawers. I heard a key in the lock and paused. Then Sandra Dennison stepped into the room, a key chain dangling from one hand and a Saturday Night Special held convincingly in the other.

"You lied to me," she said. "I know who you're working

for. Your bartender friend talks a lot."

I straightened up. "What now?"

"Now I take you out of here. Or I shoot you."

"How will you explain that?" I wanted her to keep talking; I needed time to think.

"I heard you over here in Andrea's room. I knew she was away. I came over to see who it was. You grabbed me, tried to rape me. I shot you in self-defense."

"And the gun?"

"It's not registered. I'll tell the police you brought it with you."

"Nice," I said. I didn't mention the .45 under my left armpit.

A smile toyed at the corners of Sandra's mouth. Somehow she didn't look as pretty as she had a few hours earlier.

Sandra stepped back and motioned me out of Andrea's room, down the hall, and into the stairwell. She stayed well back, out of reach, and matched my pace as we walked down the stairs.

"How much were you supposed to pay Andrea for the files?" I asked.

"Three thousand," Sandra said. "She wanted the money for her honeymoon."

"Who're you working for?" I asked, naming a pair of rival electronics firms.

Sandra didn't respond.

"What went wrong?" I squeezed one eye shut; it was a trick I'd learned as a kid.

"She was stupid," Sandra said from behind me. "It was a simple job as she blew it."

"How?"

"Andrea should have made copies. I didn't ask for the originals."

I thought about it. Every department had a copy counter on their photocopying machines and every copy had to be accounted for. It was probably easier to take the original files out of the building and copy them at the public library. I didn't tell Sandra Dennison that.

"Where is she now?"

"It doesn't matter," Sandra said. "I don't think anybody will find the body."

The answer surprised me; corporate espionage should be a gentleman's sport.

I opened the door at the bottom of the stairs and stepped into the darkened basement. Sandra followed me. I opened both eyes. It wasn't much, but I had a momentary advantage over Sandra; one eye was already prepared for darkness.

I sidestepped and spun around. The gun roared. There wasn't time to reach for the pistol under my left arm pit. I reached out, grabbed a handful of material, and tore the sleeve off her blouse. The gun roared again. I felt searing pain in my right arm. My ears reverberated with the sound. I swung my left arm in a roundhouse punch. It connected with Sandra's chin. She stumbled backward but remained standing. For a split second I admired her. Then she planted a heavy foot against my inner thigh.

I threw myself forward, crashing against her and pinning her against the concrete wall. Her heavy breasts were mashed against my chest. I caught Sandra's right wrist with my left hand. She hit me in the face with her left hand, raking my cheek with her sharp nails. I tried to block her blows with my right arm, but it wouldn't respond. The next time she brought her left hand up to hit me, I opened my mouth. I caught two of her fingers between my teeth and bit. She screamed then. I slammed her right hand against the concrete wall. The revolver clattered to the basement floor. I couldn't see where it went.

Sandra jerked her hand from my mouth. I tasted blood: I couldn't tell if it was hers or mine. She brought her knee up into my groin. I doubled over and stepped back. She'd hurt me, but I stayed on my feet.

When she came at me again, I felt the sharp bite of a knife as it sliced down my unguarded right arm. I'd never been a hero, but at that moment I realized she'd made a choice: it was going to be her life or mine.

I backed up, keeping her dark shadow in front of me, until my back was pressed against the shelves that bisected the basement. I reached behind me, grabbed a plastic box, and threw it at Sandra. She swore when it hit her. I reached behind me again and wrapped my fingers around the handle of a hammer.

Sandra rushed forward then, the knife in front of her. I swung the hammer with my left hand. The blade of her knife bit into my side. The hammer smashed into Sandra's temple and stuck. She crumpled to the floor.

I took a few ragged breaths, then stumbled across the basement, up the stairs to the lobby. Two attractive women sat on one of the couches. One of them saw me and screamed. The scrawny little desk clerk spun around. He reached under the counter for his revolver. Before he had it trained on me, I shouted, "Call the police you little shit, there's a dead woman in the basement."

Then I collapsed.

Two days later I sat in the Pink Flamingo with Charlie Fischer and Max Drummond.

"The feds filled me in yesterday at the hospital," I told them. I was nursing a beer with my left hand. "Sandra Dennison was German, working with the Iraquis. The files she got were for a missile guidance system – looked like a damn microwave to me."

"And Andrea?" Drummond asked.

"She just wanted to start the marriage off right," I said. "She wanted a honeymoon in Florida. That's all." I'd already told him Andrea was dead.

Drummond looked down at his beer. He hadn't taken a drink yet and the head was slowly disappearing. "I promised you my savings if you found out what happened to her. It was going to be the down payment on a house, but it doesn't matter now." He glanced up at me. "I owe you."

I shook my head. "You could buy the next round."

Lucky Seven

"And then he went over to Eddie's – you know, the bar over on 58th, near Washington – and he saw her with Kowalski and he got mad – mad at her or mad at him, I don't know – but he went home and he got his gun – one of those Dirty Harry guns – and –"

"A .44?"

"No, I don't think so, maybe a .357. So he got his gun and he went back to Eddie's and they were still there – sitting at the end of the bar washing each other's tongues, you know – and he shot 'em. Five, six shots – I don't know, nobody counted until it was all over and the cops showed up – but they were dead." Skinny Reeves swallowed hard. "Kowalski was a good guy – never figured him for the type to be slipping it to some other guy's wife – but I guess he won't be buying drinks no more."

"And Martini?"

"I ain't heard. He shot 'em and then he left – maybe he went home and got his stuff or maybe he had it with him when he went back to Eddie's with his gun – but nobody's seen him since he walked out of the bar."

"They sure it was Martini?"

"Seven eye witnesses – ain't one of 'em using a seeing

eye dog – so you got to believe it was him that done the shooting. They all seen him pull the trigger."

Seven people saw Joe Martini kill his wife and his best friend. Against these odds, the size of Martini's cash advance – slipped to me under the table of a greasy spoon the previous evening when we'd met to discuss his situation – seemed even smaller.

Skinny licked his lips nervously; his gaze darted from my face to the shot of Johnny Walker Red I had captured in my fist. "That's everything I heard – I swear it is."

I slid the shot glass along the bar toward Skinny. He grabbed it with both hands, brought it to his thick lips, and downed it in one gulp.

"Thanks, Nate," he said. "I appreciate it. I really do."

I pushed myself off the torn vinyl bar stool. As I turned toward the door, Skinny grabbed my sleeve.

"Do anything else for you, Nate?" he asked. "Anything at all. You just ask me and I'll do it. Okay?"

"If I need anything, I'll let you know."

"That's all I ask," Skinny said as his gnarled fist slid away from my sleeve. "I can't ask for anything more, now can I?"

I left Skinny mumbling to himself at the bar and made my way outside, pushing through the heavy wooden door from the dank interior of The Do Step Inn to the blindingly bright mid-afternoon sunlight glinting off shop windows and chrome bumpers.

I paused long enough to slip on a pair of Raybans, then headed north on 56th toward Washington. Eight blocks taken leisurely, then two blocks east on Washington to the intersection with 58th. Eddie's – the third door on the left headed north away from the intersection – had a yellow police ribbon stretched across the door frame.

"Ain'tcho heard?" one of the neighborhood kids asked as he looked up at me from where he sat in the building's shade. A comic book lay open on his knees. "Somebody done kilt somebody in there."

"I heard."

"You a cop?"

I shook my head.

Apparently, I gave the kid the wrong answer because he returned his attention to the comic book and began reading, forming words with his mouth, but not quite reading aloud. I cupped my hands over my eyes and tried to stare in through the amber glass square covering most of the top third of the door. I saw only shadows of shadows.

"They gonna open up agin tonight," the kid said without looking up. "Come back later the doors'll be open."

"What time?"

He shrugged, his thin shoulders rising and falling under his over-sized grey sweatshirt.

"What's your name?" I asked.

"Joey." He finally looked back up at me. "What's yours?"

"Nathaniel," I said. "Nathaniel Rose. My friends call me Nate."

An unmarked patrol car slid smoothly to a stop at the curb and a grossly overweight cop slid from behind the wheel.

"What the hell are you doing here?" O'Shannon asked.

"Just visiting a friend."

He looked down at Joey.

"Me and Nate was talkin bout stuff."

"Yeah?"

Joey held up his comic book. "Ninja Turtles."

"Why you interested in this?" O'Shannon asked me. As he spoke, he dug in his jacket pocket and came up with a half-flattened Milky Way bursting out of its wrapper.

"Just curious."

"It's open-and-shut. The perp's been made, we just have to find him." He peeled back the wrapper of his Milky

Way and took half the bar into his mouth before severing it. As he chewed, O'Shannon stripped the yellow police ribbon from the door frame, then pulled out a key and opened the door. He fumbled for the light switch as I followed him into the bar. Joey followed me.

At the end of the bar, dried blood and chalk outlines of the dead remained.

"Jeez," Joey said.

O'Shannon realized the kid had followed us in and was about to chase Joey out when I stopped him. "Leave the kid be."

He grumbled, then looked down at Joey. "Just stay the hell outta the way, okay?"

The kid swallowed hard, then stepped back.

"Why you down here?" I asked.

"Last chance. They're opening back up tonight."

"I heard," I said. "You think you missed something?"

"Not likely. We've got all the photos and fingerprints and blood samples and eyewitnesses we'll ever need. I just wanted one last look around." He took the last half of the Milky Way into his mouth and spoke around it. "This could be my last case. I don't want anything to go wrong."

"You a short-timer?"

"Twenty-seven years last Wednesday," he said. "And sixty-eight pounds overweight. I tried to lose the weight, but it didn't do any good. Took off twenty, put ten right back on. Mandatory retirement."

We were silent for a moment, each lost in our own little worlds, then O'Shannon laughed and said, "But what the hell, maybe it's time I got out, found another line of work."

"Like what?" I asked. "All you've ever been is a cop."

"You looking for a partner?"

The only partner I'd ever had since opening my own place had tried to kill me. I shook my head.

"Didn't think you were. Just asking."

I nosed around the bar for a few minutes, poking at the bottles. I didn't see anything I thought would be important, but right then I didn't know what important would be.

"What were they drinking?"

"Beer. They had a pitcher, about half gone. They expected to be here a while."

That reminded me of one of our best snitches.

"Skinny's out of detox," I said. "He fell off the wagon already." The shot of Johnny Walker Red I'd given him hadn't helped him climb back on, either.

"He needs somebody to watch out for him."

"Like family," I said. "Too bad he hasn't got any."

A chair fell over behind us, startling me.

As soon as we turned, Joey said, "Sorry." He lay flat on his back, still sort-of sitting in the chair. "I leaned back too far."

I helped him untangle himself from the chair, then O'Shannon handed him the comic book he'd flung halfway across the tavern when he went over backwards.

"I'm done here," O'Shannon said. "You?"

I nodded. There really wasn't anything to see. We hustled Joey out and O'Shannon locked the door. As Joey walked down the street, O'Shannon watched the kid's receding back.

"Kid like that; neighborhood like this." O'Shannon shook his head. "Somebody oughtta do something."

"You're starting to sound like a social worker."

O'Shannon snorted. "When my hemorrhoids turn to gold."

In his office half an hour later, O'Shannon said, "Your client should've gotten himself a lawyer, not a P.I."

"I suggested that to him. He said he wouldn't need a

lawyer, not if I did my job right."

O'Shannon opened a file folder on his desk. The top sheet was a witness list I shouldn't have access to. Then he said, "I gotta take a leak. I'll be back in a few minutes."

While he was gone, I quickly jotted names, phone numbers, and addresses into my notebook. I had just slid my notebook back into my jacket pocket when O'Shannon returned. He carried a Milky Way bar and was peeling back the wrapper.

"So where were we?" he asked.

"Scene of the crime," I said. "Seven witnesses, no motive."

"We got motive," O'Shannon said. "Jealous husband. If he'd caught them in the act, it might even be justifiable homicide."

"But he didn't."

"So we got premeditated. He's going down big for this one if we ever catch up to him." O'Shannon bit the Milky Way in half, then spoke as he chewed. "You know where he is, you better let on pretty fast or I'll have you in here for harboring a fugitive."

"I've only seen him once," I said. That was the night he'd hired me. I'd spoken to him on the phone twice since then, but I had instructed him not to tell me where he phoned from. "Before I knew you were interested."

Two days later I sat with Eddie Jackson, owner and primary bartender of the bar where Martini's wife and lover had died. At first, he didn't tell me anything I hadn't already heard from the other six witnesses. We sat on bar stools at the end of the bar nearest the door.

"I was looking right at the man when he pulled the trigger," he said. "There wasn't no mistake."

"How well did you know Martini?"

"He stopped by every couple of weeks, you know. Often enough so's I recognized the face, but I don't think I ever knew his name. He was rum and Coke, never varied. Light drinker. Two, maybe three drinks, then he was gone."

"Everybody else says he came in twice that night."

"First time he comes in, he sees his old lady with Kowalski. They exchanged words, some kind of argument about a test."

"What kind of test?" I asked.

"I wasn't eavesdropping," Jackson said. "I had other customers to take care of."

"What about the test?"

"Said she'd failed and it was Kowalski's fault. She asked how he knew about the test, but I never heard his answer. He stormed out and Kowalski ordered a pitcher."

"She didn't care about the test results?"

"She seemed upset at first, but Kowalski told her it had to be a false-positive. He made some kind of joke and she laughed. Wasn't nobody in the place laughing an hour later."

"Martini came back?"

"With a big mother of a handgun. I hit the floor soon as I saw it."

"You just told me you were looking straight at the killer when he pulled the trigger."

"Martini. Yeah, I was, but I was on my way to the floor. He already had his arm extended and the gun pointed at his old lady when I turned around."

"Turned?"

"I saw the look on his old lady's face and turned to see what was wrong. That's when I saw him –"

"Martini?"

"Yeah. Martini. Standing in the doorway. He fired and I flattened at about the same time."

"So you didn't actually see him kill his wife and Kowalski?" It didn't matter. Four other witnesses had seen the whole thing. Two others watched only Martini to make sure he didn't point the gun their way.

"No, I guess I didn't. I just saw that first shot, but I heard the rest." Jackson scratched his head. "I didn't get up until it was over. Until I was sure it was over."

I thanked Jackson for his time and asked how business was doing.

"The first night I opened back up, the place was crowded. You know, everybody wanting to see the spot and all. Kept my behind humping, it did. Last night, though, usual crowd."

I didn't have good news to report to my client when he phoned me at the office that evening. I'd waited around until long after Agnes had left for the day and was just about to head out for dinner when the phone rang.

That's when Martini told me the entire story.

The next afternoon, I sat on the bar stool where Martini's wife had been when he'd gunned her down. O'Shannon sat to my left. "My client claims self-defense."

"Not likely," O'Shannon said. "Premeditated. The victims were drinking beer in a public place."

"His wife tested HIV positive."

"AIDS?"

"He figured she would infect him," I explained. "Despite the affair, they still had a sex life."

O'Shannon dug in his pocket and came up with a half-empty package of peanut M&Ms. He offered me some. When I declined, he tilted back his head and poured all of them into his mouth. He chewed, swallowed, then asked, "Why the guy? Why Kowalski?"

"Figures Kowalski infected his wife."

"Yeah, maybe he did." O'Shannon pondered the universe for a moment, then said. "So we'll charge him with endangerment."

"How's that?"

"Spilled a lot of blood in that bar. Seven counts of endangerment, maybe assault with intent to kill, assault with a deadly weapon."

"The revolver?"

"His wife's blood."

The chalk outlines and the dried blood had been mostly scuffed away, but we stared down at the spot for a long time before O'Shannon said, "We've got your client stone cold. Suggest he turn himself in."

"I'll do that."

Martini hadn't hired me to prove his innocence, but to confirm his guilt, establish that the witnesses were unimpeachable, and ensure that a conviction was a sure bet. I hadn't done anything more than trace O'Shannon's footsteps, verifying the work the overweight cop had already done. Still, my client seemed satisfied.

That night when I phoned O'Shannon and told him where to find Martini, I knew he would arrive too late. My client had already acted as his own judge and jury and there would be nothing left to do but clean up the motel room where his body waited.

The Martini case was O'Shannon's last before retirement and he spent his final days on the force behind a desk, assisting younger officers with their paperwork.

The next time I saw O'Shannon, Skinny Reeves was pitching curve balls to him, and Joey and some other kids wearing green t-shirts were learning how to strike out with grace because O'Shannon couldn't hit any better than Skinny could pitch.

Despite O'Shannon's coaching, the Ninja Turtles finally won the last baseball game of the season.

Even Roses Bleed

In all my years as a Private Investigator, I'd never had a potential client walk into my office unannounced. Most phoned first to schedule an appointment, some sent letters prior to their arrival.

When Candace Wagner first stepped into my reception room, Agnes rapped on my office door, then poked her head in and told me about our visitor. "She doesn't have an appointment and she won't tell me her name."

We made Candace wait nearly fifteen minutes while we pretended to be busy. Then Agnes ushered her into my office, seated her in the hard-backed chair across the desk from mine, and prepared mugs of coffee for us.

I examined my potential client carefully. Except for a prominent Adam's apple, she was my idea of the perfect woman: long blonde hair flowing in gentle waves to her shoulders, emerald green eyes and pouting red lips, minimal make-up, a white silk blouse cut so low I thought I could get lost for days in her cleavage, a knee-length black wool skirt with wide pleats, dark hose, black pumps with a modest heel. A few years younger than me and a few inches shorter. The type of woman I could fall for. The type of woman I had fallen for many times before.

After introductions, I asked Candace what she thought I could do for her. I took a sip of coffee and waited for her answer.

"I want you to kill my husband."

I almost spit out my coffee. After I recovered, I asked, "Why me?"

"I like your name," she said. "I like roses."

"Found my name in the phone book and just came in, is that it?"

She smiled. "Mannie Goldstein mentioned your name."

"How do you know Mannie?"

She told me about the west county alcoholic rehabilitation center owned by Mannie's brother-in-law and how her husband had spent time there.

"So you're married to an alkie?"

"Recovering alcoholic," she corrected. "He takes life one day at a time, now."

"What's he do when he isn't recovering?"

She looked me a question.

"He got a job?"

"Investments," she said. "That's what he tells me."

"Pretty vague."

"He inherited his Granddaddy's money. He doesn't have to work."

I understood.

"He beat you? Fool around? Got a lot of insurance?"

"Why?"

"Need a reason to want him dead."

"So you'll do it?"

I shook my head. The only time I'd ever killed that wasn't self-defense was when a local Mafioso murdered Julie Bronski, the first woman I'd slept with after my wife Lydie's death. I wasn't proud of what I'd done, but I knew I'd do it all over again if things shook out the same way. And they probably would since both Lydie and Julie had been clients before they'd become lovers.

"Maybe you're not the man Goldstein said you were."

Candace stood and I stood. She thanked me, then I ushered her to the door and watched as she walked down the hall to the elevator.

I closed the door, then turned to face Agnes. My three-room, second-floor office wasn't in the most prestigious building, but I'd ensured that no one could tell from the inside. Agnes sat before a print that cost more than my first year's income, fluorescent light reflecting dully from her ebony skin.

Agnes looked at me expectantly. "You take the job?"

I told her why I hadn't.

Two days later Agnes handed me the morning paper when I arrived at the office, already folded open to the story on page two about the death of a local businessman named Phillip Wagner. The fourth graph of the story named his widow, the former Candace Stevens, and I knew I had a phone call to make.

Phillip's grieving widow answered on the third ring. When I told her I'd have to visit the police to tell them what I knew, she implored me not to.

"I need to talk to you first," she said. "Come to the house."

"When?" I asked.

"As soon as you can get here." She gave me the address.

As soon as I could get there turned out to be thirty-two minutes after she disconnected the line, much of the time taken up by walking to the garage where I'd left my Corvette. Candace answered the door when I rang the bell, opening it promptly.

The grieving widow wore black – a lacy see-through

number that left nothing to the imagination and proved that she was a natural blonde. I eyed her up and down, enjoying the view but wondering why she'd given it to me.

"You could have dressed," I said.

She said, "I did."

I stepped inside and pushed the heavy wooden door closed behind me, then followed her into the living room where she sat on a white sofa, one leg tucked under her. I sat across from her.

"I didn't kill him," she said.

"But you wanted him dead."

"You'll have to believe me." She didn't implore or beg. She just said it flat out. "Somebody beat me to it. I want to know who."

"What about the police?"

"They think I did it."

"Why?"

"You read the paper," she said. "What did it say?"

"Your husband was shot to death yesterday evening outside the Swankton Theater."

"You know where I was? Right here. Alone. I haven't an alibi." She licked her pouting red lips with the tip of her tongue, then shifted her legs, parting them slightly. I tried to concentrate my attention on her face.

"So the police came down hard on you?"

"Phillip's estate is worth about two million, his life insurance is worth another million. Except for a hundred thousand going to the rehab center that dried him out, the rest is mine. They tell me I've got nearly three million motives."

"Sounds that way."

"But I didn't do it, and I didn't have it done."

"And what do you want from me?"

"I want you to find Phillip's killer."

"You want justice?"

She smiled. "If that's what you want to call it," she said. "I just want to be sure my next home doesn't have two bunks and bars on the window."

"Prison's not a nice place to spend time."

"So," Candace said, "a retainer for your services to make it all proper." She offered me a check for ten thousand dollars. She'd made it out before my arrival and it had waited on the end table until that moment. I had no reason to believe her story, but I took the check, folded it in half, and slipped it into my shirt pocket.

I stood to leave, then she stood. We walked to the front door, then stopped. I had my hand on the knob, about to twist it open. She stopped me, one hand covering mine. Then she pressed herself against me, molding her body to mine and wrapping one arm around the back of my head to pull my face down to hers.

She kissed me and I returned the kiss, our mouths meeting in a predatory coupling that was hard and wet and took away my breath. I released the doorknob and wrapped my arms around her, pulling her body tight against mine, feeling her quiver against me.

I wanted her and she knew it. Right then. Right there. But I pushed her away, holding her at arm's length.

"What's wrong, Nate?" she whispered.

I didn't answer. Instead, I opened the door and stepped outside. As I walked to the car, I pulled my handkerchief out and tried to wipe away the lipstick that covered my face. I wanted the soldier in my pants to quit standing at attention before I returned to the office, so I took the long way back.

When I returned to the office, I endorsed the check and gave it to Agnes. She looked at the amount written on the face and whistled. "That's going to pay a lot of bills," she said. "What does it buy?"

I couldn't tell her because I didn't know. Even if Candace hadn't been involved in the death of her husband, there remained a good chance she could be convicted of conspiracy to commit murder if I took my story to the cops. Ten thousand could buy a lot of silence, if I had it to sell.

A moment later, I dropped into the chair behind my desk, reached for the phone, and dialed O'Shannon's home number. He answered halfway through the first ring. After identifying myself, I asked if he wanted to make some extra money.

He asked what he had to do.

"I can't be in two places at once," I told him. He'd only been retired a short time and I needed him to spend time with some of his former buddies in Homicide. "See what you can dig up about the Wagner murder."

"What's in it for me?"

I named an hourly figure that he found acceptable. After I disconnected the call with O'Shannon, I phoned Mannie Goldstein's house and left a message on his machine. I wanted to know what he might have heard about Phillip Wagner's stay at his brother-in-law's rehab center. After leaving the message for Mannie, I took a walk.

A jalopy rental operation had an office at the garage where I kept my Corvette and I rented a non-descript blue Ford. I drove it back to the Wagner's neighborhood and parked on the street where I could watch the entrance to Candace's home. The police came and went, a pair of plainclothes officers in an unmarked car who spent half-an-hour inside with Candace. After they departed, the postman walked up the drive and stuffed the mailbox full. A few minutes later, a Mercedes backed out of the garage. I followed it to the horse track, where the driver parked near the stable. A little guy walked up to the window and spoke to the driver for ten minutes, becoming increasingly agitated until he finally stalked away. Then the Mercedes returned to the garage at the Wagner residence. Although I never got close enough to the Mercedes to see the driver's face, I presumed it was Candace because I had not seen anyone else enter or leave her house. Nothing else happened for the next three hours, so I returned to the office.

There I spent the next half-hour completing a written report for another client, a woman who suspected her new boyfriend of being something other than what he presented himself as. Her suspicions had been correct since the guy had a wife and family in San Francisco and another in St. Paul. I'd already given Francine Dierman an oral overview so nothing in my report should surprise her. When I completed everything, I gave it to Agnes to copy and mail along with an invoice for my time.

O'Shannon arrived and joined me in my office.

"They found Wagner in the alley behind the Swankton. One shot through the heart at close range," O'Shannon reported. He'd arrived with a sack of Barnburgers and fries gripped in one hand and he ate at my desk while we spoke. "No signs of a struggle. He must have known the killer to go into an alley with him and let him get that close without a struggle."

"What else?" I asked. I pulled a pad and pen from my desk drawer and began taking notes.

"The killer used a .38. They recovered the slug but not the casing."

"Suspects?"

"Only the wife so far." O'Shannon stopped long enough to take a huge bite from the remaining Barnburger, then he continued. "There's no witnesses to the murder. Only the ticket-taker at the Swankton remembers seeing Wagner, but she says he only bought one ticket and he went in alone."

"What time?"

"Show started at five o'clock, one of those commuter

specials." When I looked him a question, O'Shannon said. "A couple of the theaters downtown offer early shows. Get off work, see a show, then drive home to the burbs after rush hour's ended. Cuts twenty to thirty minutes off the driving time."

Agnes brought a mug of coffee in and placed it near my right hand. Then she exited as quietly as she'd entered.

"He stay for the entire show?"

"The movie ended at 6:49, his body was discovered at 7:10."

"Who found it?" I sipped at the coffee.

"One of the ushers, an acne-faced kid named Wilson Goodrich. The Swankton is a multiplex. He and the other ushers clean out the theaters between shows and he was wheeling one of the big canisters out back to the dumpster when he saw the body. He reported it right away, uniforms were on the scene by 7:15, Homicide and the crime lab within the next ten minutes. Everything by the book, right down the line. They found Wagner's wallet in his pocket and identified him immediately."

"Why they pick up on the wife as a suspect?"

"The dead guy's worth about three mil and she says she was home alone." O'Shannon gobbled down a handful of greasy fries. "They talked to her for about two hours, but didn't get anywhere. They say she's cool as a cucumber. She did say one thing they thought unusual."

"What's that?"

"When they first notified her of her husband's death, Mrs. Wagner said, 'He deserved it.' She wouldn't elaborate or explain what she meant."

When O'Shannon finished his report, he said, "How much longer you going to need me?"

I didn't know and I told him so.

"I can't work out of my apartment. I ain't set up for it."

Agnes and I had turned Stu Callason's office into a store

room after his death. My first and only partner had turned out to be a double-crossing blackmailer and I had not had any desire to take on another partner. Still, O'Shannon needed a place to keep a few files and make a few phone calls, so we pushed things out of the way, cleaned up Callason's old desk, and let O'Shannon use the office. Agnes found a duplicate office key so he could keep his own hours.

While O'Shannon was arranging his desk, Mannie returned my call. When I told him what I wanted, he said, "Meet me at Charlie Fischer's place in half an hour. We can talk there."

Charlie had a bar on the near-north side and he'd served as a reliable source of information more than once over the years.

Before leaving, I gave O'Shannon the keys to the rented Ford and told him to stakeout the Wagner home. "And don't leave candy wrappers all over the car, either."

I beat Mannie by three minutes and Charlie had already set me up with a draft beer. Charlie's a slender guy with a pencil-thin mustache waxed to a point at each end and black hair greased straight back from his forehead to his shirt collar.

"You don't make many social calls," Charlie said, "so you must be working. Got a big case?"

"Murder."

He whistled. "Big enough."

Mannie bustled in just as I took my first sip from the beer mug. He's a short guy with a ring of nappy black hair surrounding the bald crown of his head, with a plump face and sagging jowls.

We sat together at the far end of the bar after Charlie shooed a couple of other patrons away.

"All this is on the Q.T., right?" Mannie asked. His thin, high-pitched voice sounded like he'd never graduated from puberty.

"Of course," I told him.

"Okay, here's what I got." He looked around before continuing. "Phillip Wagner spent last July at my brother-in-law's place. He showed up on the Fifth after what must have been one hell of a bender on the Fourth. His old lady only visited him once, and from what I heard, they must have had one hell of an argument because she stormed out of there like nobody's business. The last thing anybody heard her say was, 'I'll kill you before I'll let you do that to me.'"

Charlie brought a draft beer for Mannie.

"Anybody know what she was talking about?"

"Nobody."

I took another direction with my questions. "Phillip legit?"

"Mostly," Manny said. "He inherited a bit of money from his grandfather and he parlayed it into more. There's word that he's spread a good deal of it around the track."

"He likes the ponies?"

"He did. He dropped four thousand last weekend."

"He into any bookies?"

"Not that I've heard."

"You hear anything else, you let me know." I saw Charlie's ear cocked in our direction, so I included him in on the arrangement. Then I drained my beer, dropped a fifty on the counter for Mannie and a five for the beers before leaving.

I drove to the Wagner home, stopping outside to talk to O'Shannon before continuing up the drive. Candace had had no visitors since his arrival and as far as O'Shannon knew, she was the only person inside the home. I confirmed his assumption when I rang the bell and she answered.

"I wasn't expecting company," she said as she ushered me inside. "Or I'd have been prepared."

She had pulled her hair back in a pony tail and she wore loose-fitting sweatpants and a sweatshirt. It didn't matter what she wore, I already knew what was underneath.

I sat on one end of the couch, she sat on the other.

I got right to the point. "I know about the argument you had with Phillip at the rehab center. You threatened to kill him."

Candace didn't seem surprised, but she said, "I had forgotten all about that."

"What were you arguing about?"

"He threatened to divorce me."

"That all?"

"Isn't that enough?"

"A good lawyer would have gotten you half this stuff."

"I signed a prenuptual agreement. Maybe it would hold up in court, maybe it wouldn't, but it limited me to two hundred thousand if we divorced."

"Good reason to have him killed," I said. "Do the police know about this yet?"

"They haven't said anything."

"And you still insist you had nothing to do with Phillip's death."

"I've never denied that I wanted him dead," she said. "But I swear I had nothing to do with his death."

She slid down the couch and sat so close I could feel the body heat radiating off of her.

"How can I convince you I'm telling the truth?" she asked just before her lips covered mine. Then my hands were up under her sweatshirt and I could tell that she was as excited as I was.

Our clothes came off and our bodies came together, fitting as if designed just for one another. It was hard and wet and sloppy and it took my breath away and still she wanted more.

Before long I gave it to her.

"You were in there a long time," O'Shannon said when I pulled alongside the rented Ford later that night. He had a Milky Way in one hand and a diet cola in the other.

"We had things to talk about. After all, she's paying the freight on this one."

"I'm sure she is," O'Shannon said. As I dropped my Corvette back into gear, O'Shannon said, "One more thing."

"Yeah?"

"Wipe the lipstick off your face."

Instead of going to my apartment, I drove back to the office and sat at my desk looking over my notes. I had the feeling I was missing something, something important, and I wasn't sure what it was. I looked over all my notes again.

I'd learned a good deal about Phillip Wagner but I knew next to nothing about Candace. I phoned Mannie and said, "Find out everything you can about Candace Wagner, maiden name Stevens. Get back to me as soon as possible."

He said he would and rang off.

Then I went home, slept for a few hours, then drove back to Candace's house. I replaced O'Shannon on the stakeout, letting him take my Corvette. I let him take a six hour break and nothing happened during my stay in the rented Ford.

When O'Shannon returned, he brought with him three sacks of breakfast food from Burgerbarn. He offered to share, but I graciously excused myself. I went home, showered, changed clothes, and went into the office. Agnes had already settled in behind her desk.

"I paid rent two months ahead," she said, "and I brought the electrical bill up to date. There's still five thousand left in the account."

I thanked her and headed into my office, closing the door. I called around, trying to get a lead onto Phillip Wagner. It turned out I knew a few people who knew a few people.

Most of them confirmed what O'Shannon had already told me. Wagner played the horses, often dropping some big bucks. He also had a habit of cashing in big by betting on horses that really should not have had any reasonable expectation of winning.

"He's got a thing with a couple of jockeys," one source told me, but no one else could confirm his comments.

Another mentioned that Wagner lost fifty g's only a week before when his horse came up lame in the first turn. The source said, "It wasn't like Wagner to lose the really big bets."

Nothing anyone told me implicated Candace.

I felt certain that Candace had nothing to do with her husband's murder and I visited her the next evening to tell her so. She met me at the door wearing a lacy baby-doll. She'd dimmed the lights and had classical music playing softly on the stereo.

I told her what I'd come to tell her, but it only took a few minutes. After that, our lips fastened together with a hungry passion that didn't need words and she led me upstairs to the bedroom where we stripped off each other's clothes, fell into bed, and began the erotic merging of two bodies into one.

"You double-crossing bitch," said a voice I didn't recognize.

I looked over my shoulder and saw a little guy brandishing a snub-nosed .38, the business end pointed at my backside and ready to give me a lead enema. I rolled off of

Candace, my amorous interest suddenly deflated.

I recognized the guy with the gun as the little guy I'd seen at the track the day before. I tried to ask him a question, but he wasn't interested in conversation. He squeezed off two shots, both aimed at Candace, and I came up out of the bed in a flash, diving toward him as he turned the revolver on me.

I heard a third gun shot, then the little guy's chest erupted in a fountain of blood that sprayed across Candace's bedroom.

"I saw him sneaking in, so I followed him," O'Shannon said as he reholstered his Police Special. "I didn't figure him to be up to any good."

I turned to look at Candace as she came up out of the bed and practically fell into my arms. The little guy had been a lousy shot and both bullets had embedded themselves in the plaster wall about a foot above where Candace's head had been.

"What did he want?" I looked from Candace to O'Shannon.

O'Shannon retrieved my pants from the floor and tossed them toward me. I caught them one-handed, my other arm still wrapped around Candace.

"Get dressed," O'Shannon said as he reached for the phone. "The cops'll be here any minute."

It took a couple of days for the cops to sort through everything, but it turned out that the little guy was Petey Johnson, a jockey who'd thrown a few races for Phillip Wagner and the two slugs the cops dug out of the wall in Candace's bedroom matched the one that killed Phillip. Another jockey claimed he'd overheard Petey and Phillip arguing about money the day before Phillip's death, and the cops figured the little guy had been stiffed.

"Why'd he break into the house?" one of the cops asked me during routine questioning.

The police didn't have any idea why the jockey had tried to kill Candace and me, and O'Shannon hadn't arrived in time to hear the little guy's last words. I told the homicide cop I had a theory so he told me to give it a spin.

"Look, he expect some big money from Phillip Wagner, big enough that he killed Wagner over it. But with Wagner dead, he still didn't have the loot. He probably figured there was a way to get it from the grieving widow."

The cops had their killer and they had a motive that satisfied them, so they wrapped up the case in a neat bundle and tossed it to the D.A. The D.A.'s office had better things to do than prosecute dead guys, so they tossed the whole bundle into a file drawer somewhere.

While the cops were wrapping things up, I offered O'Shannon a full-time gig and he accepted. Any guy that can cover my backside the way he had deserved to hang around on a permanent basis.

Still, something about the way things had strung out bugged me, and I couldn't put it all together until Mannie met me two weeks later in a back booth at Charlie Fischer's bar.

"I finally got the dope on Candace Wagner," he said in that annoying whine of his.

"A little too late, isn't it?" I asked. "The case is closed."

"I thought you'd want to know anyhow," Mannie said. "Since you've been spending so much time with the widow and all."

"So spill it."

"They met in Louisville, Kentucky, a long time ago. He was down at the Derby that year. Only here's the thing. Back then Candace Stevens was known as Carl Stevens." He slid an envelope from his jacket pocket, opened it and pulled out copies of Carl's birth certificate, hospital admission records, and a copy of the surgeon's report detailing the operation. I didn't ask how he'd obtained everything, and I doubt he would have told me if I had asked. "Phillip paid for the operation and they got married a year later. I tumbled to all this when I located the alkie who stayed in the room next to Phillip's last July. He heard the entire argument. He said Phillip threatened to divorce Candace and reveal the details of her operation at the same time. The alkie didn't think much about it when it happened since he was going through a bad case of the D.T.s at the time." Mannie smiled. "Three fingers of Jack from a fresh bottle loosened his tongue pretty damned quick."

"You pushed him off the wagon?"

Mannie laughed. "Got to keep my brother-in-law in business or he'll send my sister back."

I scooped up everything and left him sitting alone in the booth.

"Hey," he called after me as I headed for the door. "That stuff cost me a bundle."

"Send me a bill," I called over my shoulder.

I drove directly to Candace's home.

"You're early," she said when she answered the door. She wore a powder blue robe that she held closed with one hand. "Dinner's not even ready yet and I haven't dressed."

"I'm not hungry," I told her.

Candace wrapped one arm around the back of my neck and stretched up to kiss me. I pushed her away and the robe fell open. What I saw contradicted what Mannie had told me. No doctor could do a job that good.

"What's wrong?" Candace asked. "What's gotten into you?"

I repeated Mannie's story. She didn't deny any of it.

"You don't hate me, do you?" She let the robe slip off her shoulders and it fell to the floor. No surgeon is that good,

I thought again. Then I saw her Adam's apple bob up and down.

I didn't answer her question. Instead, I asked one of my own. "Did Petey Johnson know about this?"

"What's that little weasel got to do with this?"

"You set him up, didn't you? What did you promise him for killing Phillip? What was his angle?"

"I think it's time you left," Candace said.

I did, walking out of her house with a wad of crumpled paper in my hand. I climbed into the Corvette and drove for hours, turning everything over and over in my head.

Candace had used me like she had used Petey Johnson. Paid me ten thousand dollars to prove she couldn't have been involved in her husband's murder, and when I did prove it she strung me out a while longer, just to make sure the story played the way she wanted it to. I couldn't go to the cops without implicating myself and she knew it.

Did I love her or did I hate her?

Damned if I knew.

A month later, after she'd sold the house and moved to the British West Indies, Candace sent me a dozen roses. The delivery boy left them outside my office door one afternoon when Agnes had the day off. By the time I returned, they'd wilted in the heat.

I tried to phone Candace, but she never returned my calls again.

Tequila Sunrise and the Horse

The young blonde known as Lime Ricky sat to my right, facing me. Her right knee pressed against my right knee, her left knee pressed against the fleshy part of my right butt cheek. She leaned slightly forward, her left hand braced on the back of my chair, her right hand unzipping my fly.

She resisted when I tried to push her hand away, her fingers burrowing through the twisted cloth of my underwear. I stared hard into her eyes and pushed her hand away a second time. The blonde finally released her grip on me, then slid the twenty from the table, rolled it into a thin tube, and slipped it between her sweaty breasts into her bra.

As she stood to leave, I caught her wrist, my thick fingers easily encircling it. "Sit."

Lime Ricky looked a hard question at me until I placed a second twenty on the table.

"You're not ready to do it again."

"Just talk," I said.

"You have to buy me a drink."

I motioned for one of the waitresses with my free hand, had her refill my beer and bring a vodka tonic for my reluctant guest. When Lime Ricky finally sat, I released my hold on her wrist.

She made the second twenty disappear into her cleavage. "So talk."

"You know Tequila Sunrise?"

The blonde stood abruptly, knocking her chair backward. I caught her wrist again.

"She's dead."

"Sit," I said. "Finish your drink."

She glared hard at me. One of the bouncers noticed and began to thread his way toward our table. Lime Ricky waved him away, then righted her chair. She slowly eased into it.

"Who are you?"

"Rose," I said. "Nathaniel Rose. Her parents hired me."

"I don't know anything," the blonde insisted.

I lifted my beer.

"Drink," I said. When she lifted her vodka tonic, I added, "To good health and long life."

"That a crack?" Lime Ricky asked. "Tequila Sunrise didn't see twenty-two."

The names made me sick. At the owner's insistence, all the dancers in the bar used drink names as their stage names, and I'd already talked my way through enough drinks to give me a hangover the next morning.

The only thing I'd learned from any of the girls, despite having shelled out too many twenties, was the reason for the stupid names. It was so cheating spouses could honestly tell inquisitive wives that they'd "stopped for a drink after work."

After I finished my beer, I laid my business card on the table with another twenty. Lime Ricky picked them both up, rolled the card inside the twenty, and made them disappear between her breasts with the other money I'd given her.

I talked to two more girls at The Drinking Fountain before heading over to The Kitty Kat Klub, where Inez Ortiz had danced under the name The Hot Tamale – an even more derogatory reference to her Mexican heritage.

I learned nothing of value at either place and feared reporting back to her parents that I had done no better than the disinterested detectives who had been assigned the case when Tequila's body had been found behind a dumpster in the alley between Fourth and Fifth Streets.

I returned to my office, knocked back a pair of antacids to stop the rumbling in my stomach, and spent the next hour paying bills and preparing invoices for other clients. It seemed the more successful my P.I. business became, the less time I had to do any actual detecting.

I finished my paperwork, then went home, showered, and dropped into bed a few minutes before midnight.

The phone rang at three a.m., rousing me from a pleasant dream involving two excessively-endowed blonde wrestlers and a tub of lime Jello. I rolled onto my side, my erection acting like a bicycle kickstand and preventing me from going further, and reached for the phone.

"Yuh," I said, still groggy.

"Rose?" A female voice, young and familiar.

"Yeah." I sat up and swung my legs off the side of the bed. Pressing the soles of my feet against the cold wooden floor woke me faster than the motor-oil-thick coffee at Mac's Diner on Seventh.

"I know what you're looking for."

"Who is this?"

"Sissy Ledbetter," she said. "We spoke this afternoon."

I'd spoken to a lot of women that afternoon.

"Lime Ricky," she said. "I choked your chicken at The Drinking Fountain."

"I know who you are," I told her. "My friends call me

Nate."

"Come to my apartment, Nate," she said, "and I'll show you what I've got." She gave me the address. "Come now, before I change my mind."

I dropped the phone into its cradle and pulled on a two-day-old pair of button-fly jeans, a fresh shirt, and a pair of running shoes. I made it out of the apartment in less than five minutes and within half an hour I'd parked my T-Bird in front of Sissy Ledbetter's apartment building.

She lived on the fourth floor of a six-floor walk-up and I took the steps two at a time, stopping for a moment to catch my breath before knocking on her apartment door.

A moment later I heard the dead bolt snap open, then the door opened as far as the safety chain would allow. One pale blue eye looked out at me, then the door closed again. When it reopened, the safety chain had been removed.

Sissy Ledbetter stood before me, wearing a short red silk robe loosely tied at the waist with a black sash.

I stepped inside and closed the door behind me. She snapped the deadbolt into place and slipped the safety chain back on. Then she led me down the short entryway and into the living room.

"Inez was a friend of mine," Sissy said without preamble. "What happened to her shouldn't have happened, but she got mixed up with the wrong people."

Sissy dropped onto the black leather couch and her robe slipped open for a moment. She wore nothing beneath the robe and I caught a glimpse of one ample breast and a silken puff of blonde hair at the juncture of her thighs before she pulled the robe closed again.

"If they knew I was talking to you, I don't know what they'd do to me," Sissy said. "Maybe the same thing they did to Inez."

I sat in a black leather chair directly across from Sissy. She leaned forward and pushed two Polaroid photographs across the top of the glass coffee table that separated us.

"The one on the left is Horse McCoy."

In the photo, Inez had the head of Horse's cock in her mouth and her hand wrapped around its base. It didn't take a rocket scientist to figure out how Horse had come by his name.

"The other guy is Real –"

"Real what?" I asked.

"That's his name," Sissy said. "He's Horse's older brother."

"So he's the Real McCoy?" I asked.

"Yeah," she said. "I've seen his license."

It was obvious she didn't get the joke, so I didn't push it. I asked, "Why show me pictures of these two?"

"Inez left The Drinking Fountain with the McCoys the night before her body was discovered. She didn't look happy," Sissy explained. "That's the last time I saw her."

"You tell this to the police?"

Sissy shook her head. A few wisps of blonde hair floated around her face and she brushed them away.

"How'd you come by these pictures?"

"Inez gave them to me. She said the McCoys were always taking pictures of her. She didn't figure they'd miss a few."

Sissy leaned forward and tapped on one of the photos, her finger landing on Real's face. "This is the mean one. I once saw him bitch-slap one of the bouncers at The Drinking Fountain. That night the guy quit and last I heard, he moved out of town. Horse will do anything his brother tells him to, but I don't think he's ever had an original thought."

Sissy sat back. The sash on her robe had worked loose and Sissy's robe gaped open, revealing the same breast I'd seen earlier. I looked away.

"Can I take these?" I asked, picking the two photos up from the coffee table.

When Sissy nodded, I slipped both photos into my shirt pocket, then stood to leave. She followed me to the door and when I turned back toward her, I realized that the sash on Sissy's robe had come completely undone and it lay on the floor behind her. Her robe hung open and I took full advantage of the view.

She glanced down, saw what I saw, and made no effort to close her robe.

I grabbed her then, pulling her to me.

"You've been teasing me all night," I said hoarsely. Then I wrapped one thick hand in her long, blonde hair and tilted her head back as I covered her mouth with mine.

Her lips parted, our teeth crashed together, and then our tongues met in an explosion of desire. I pressed her against the wall, leaning against her with all of my weight and feeling her heavy breasts smash against my chest. She forced her hand between us and popped open every one of the buttons on my jeans.

I wanted her right then and I didn't want to wait. I spun Sissy around and lifted the back of her robe. Then I took her from behind.

I held on so tight I thought I might bruise her, but I couldn't stop myself. I took her hard and I took her fast and she met every one of my powerful thrusts with one of her own.

Finally, after I finished, she twisted around and we kissed a long, deep, penetrating kiss. When it ended, she whispered, "Stay with me."

I didn't say anything when she took my hand and led me into the bedroom where she helped me strip off my clothes.

awoke the next morning to find Sissy sitting on the bed

beside me, staring down at me. When she realized I'd awoken, she lay back down, her head cradled in my arm, her lithe young body pressed against me. It must have been twenty minutes before she finally climbed out of bed.

I slapped her bare ass as I pushed myself upright and swung my legs off the bed. "I have to get to work."

I pulled on my clothes, rinsed my face in the bathroom, then stepped into the hall. Sissy pulled on her robe and met me at the door. She hooked one hand behind my neck and pulled my face down to hers. She kissed me, but it wasn't the same passionate kiss as the night before. It was a soft kiss, and she looked deep into my eyes as she kissed me. I don't know what she saw, but when the kiss finally ended, she said, "Find the bastards who did that to Inez."

I returned home, showered, and changed clothes. After I'd changed, I reached into the pocket of the shirt I'd worn the previous night. In addition to the two Polaroid photos Sissy had given me, I found both of the twenties I'd given her the previous day when I'd visited The Drinking Fountain.

I drove directly to the office, talked to Agnes about her and Roland's up-coming 40th wedding anniversary, then stepped into my office.

In the bottom drawer of my desk, behind some files I kept on closed cases, I found my .45 and my shoulder rig. I checked the load in the clip, checked the action, and then strapped the whole thing on. I pulled a light jacket on over everything, hoping the bulge wasn't too noticeable, and then began looking for the McCoy brothers.

The baseball team O'Shannon coached had made it to the city league playoffs and he'd taken the week off, so I had to work the case alone. I spread a few dollars among my regulars – Mannie Goldstein, Charlie Fischer, and others –

and tried to scare up the McCoy brothers.

They had dropped from sight. Even though the brothers were known by many of the bouncers, bartenders, and dancers I talked to, none admitting seeing them recently. Nearly two days passed before I found a dancer who admitted knowing where the brothers lived.

"They took me there a couple of times," she said. "It's a spooky old warehouse. They live up on the second floor. There's pictures of Inez up there. A whole wall full of them."

She gave me the address and directions.

"Don't tell them where you got the address," she said. "Don't mention my name at all."

Around 4 a.m., I found the warehouse, parked the T-Bird out of sight a block away, and then carefully circumnavigated the place. From the outside, it looked just like all the other warehouses in the neighborhood. Then I looked at the locks on the doors.

I realized subtlety wouldn't get me inside, so I returned to the T-Bird for a tire iron and used it to smash in one of the windows. Then I reached inside and unfastened a pair of deadbolts.

If anyone heard the glass breaking, they didn't respond and I was inside the warehouse and moving quietly up the steps to the second floor in a matter of moments. I had the tire iron in my left hand, my .45 in my right.

At the top of the stairs, I found a solid steel door. It had been left open a crack and I used the tire iron to push it open even further.

Then I stepped through the open doorway into the main living area, a room nearly twice the size of my entire house. The sun had just begun to rise and dim light filtered in through the skylights. I could see a fireplace at one end, three different furniture groupings, and a bar at the other end. Someone with money but without taste had put the whole thing together, but then I never would have figured the

McCoy brothers for Martha Stewart's relatives.

I kept my back to the wall as I moved down the length of the room, and stopped when something scraped my neck. I turned and found myself facing the wall of photos I'd been told about. As the morning light grew stronger, the room brightened. I examined the photos. The McCoy brothers had been fascinated with Inez, and they had photographed her in nearly every position imaginable, alone and with one or both of the brothers.

I had become so engrossed in the wall of photos that I almost didn't hear him in time. I spun around and found Horse charging at me across the room.

By the time I raised my pistol, he'd crashed into me, knocking me back against the wall of photos, causing them to rain down on us as we collapsed to the floor.

The .45 spun out of my grip across the parquet floor and I tried to beat Horse off with the tire iron. It seemed to have no effect on him and he pounded me twice in the gut and once in the side of the head before I rolled out from under him.

I lost the tire iron in my effort to get away and he picked it up. He swung at my head and I ducked. A lamp crashed to the floor. He swung again and I fell backward over an ottoman. The tire iron whistled above me.

As I scrambled to my feet, I felt the .45 on the floor and I picked it up.

I leveled it at Horse McCoy.

"Drop it!"

He glared at me, then lifted the tire iron and charged me again. I aimed at his chest and squeezed the trigger just as he knocked me backward in a diving tackle. I knew I'd missed his chest, but I didn't know where I'd hit him as I pushed out from under the big man.

He lay on the floor in a fetal position, screaming in pain.

I found a phone and dialed the police, waiting until two

officers arrived ten minutes later.

I spent most of the day at the police station, repeating my story until my face felt as blue as the police uniforms. They finally released me around dinner time. I called Sissy from the pay phone in the station's lobby, then caught a cab back to where I'd left the T-Bird.

By the time I made it home, Sissy had already arrived and she waited in the lobby with take-out Chinese. Over dinner I told her everything that had happened, and everything I'd learned since then. It was a longer version than I planned to tell Inez Ortiz's parents the next day.

Between what I told the police, what Horse told them, and what they could piece together on their own, they determined that Inez had died of natural causes – a heart attack caused by a congenital heart defect – but Real and Horse didn't know that. Real and Horse both thought Real had killed her, and they dumped her body behind the dumpster that night. Then Real made Horse remove all the evidence of Inez's presence from their home above the warehouse.

Horse did everything his brother asked until he was told to remove the wall of photos. He refused, Real bitch-slapped him, and then Horse snapped. He grabbed his older brother, broke his neck, and then stuffed him in the deep freeze where the police later found the body.

"Horse was smart enough to know that somebody would figure out they were the last people with Inez, and when I appeared in his living room he knew the jig was up," I explained around a mouthful of fried rice.

I told Sissy all about the fight and my visit to the police station afterward, concluding with, "The funny thing is, if Horse hadn't killed his brother, the worst they could have been charged with is unlawful disposal of a body."

"So where *did* you shoot him?" Sissy finally asked as she cracked open her fortune cookie.

"In the crotch," I explained, "and there's nothing left to reattach. By the time he gets to prison, he'll be known as Quarter-Horse."

Only Business

Even though I'd often seen her photo on the society page, I didn't meet Marilyn Richards until Agnes ushered her into my office one sweltering summer day.

My building's aging air conditioning struggled to move tepid air through our three rooms so I'd loosened my tie and undone my collar. Even though sweat seemed to ooze from every part of my body, Marilyn only appeared inconvenienced by the heat.

After introducing herself, she offered me a job and I listened to the details.

"It should be easy enough, Mr. Rose," she said. "Follow Bo for a few days, then tell me where he's been and what he's done."

I named my rate and she didn't blink.

"Plus expenses."

She reached into her purse and retrieved a leather-covered checkbook. "I presume you require a retainer."

Sweat beaded on my brow and I wiped it away with a handkerchief while she wrote the check. My office had been hot before Marilyn's arrival but her presence had raised the temperature another ten degrees. After she'd settled into the chair across from me, she'd crossed her long, slim legs, causing her short skirt to hike up her thighs. Now, as she leaned forward, her heavy breasts threatened to spill from her crisp, white blouse.

When Marilyn slid the completed check across the desk, I folded it in half and placed it in my shirt pocket. Then Marilyn placed a photograph on my desk. She said, "This is Bo."

Bullet-headed, Bo Delacroix had closely-cropped black hair, a single eyebrow stretched along his thick brow, and a boxer's flattened nose. He wore pointy-toed cowboy boots, tight-fitting blue jeans, and a muscle shirt. His upper arms and thick chest stretched his shirt tight enough to make the threads scream.

"You're right," I told her. "He should be easy to follow."

Marilyn told me where to find Bo, then she stood to leave. I watched her walk to the office door, open it, then turn back. She said, "Don't disappoint me."

Then she stepped through the open doorway and the door closed slowly behind her. All that remained was the faint scent of Jasmine.

I used my already-soggy handkerchief to mop my brow again, then I stared at the photo of Bo. It wasn't Marilyn's boyfriend that interested me this time, it was his surroundings.

Bo stood in an office. Behind him were a glass and chrome desk, a bookcase containing a pair of trophies, a black leather chair, the left-most portion of a law degree.

I wondered what a guy like Bo would be doing in a place like that. Then I wondered what a woman like Marilyn would be doing with a guy like Bo. The pieces didn't fit together.

When I retrieved my .45 from my desk drawer, I realized how much my life had changed since Lydie's death. Then I strapped on my shoulder holster and slid the .45 into it. I gave the retainer check to Agnes, then poked my head into O'Shannon's office. The grossly overweight ex-cop was hunched over his computer keyboard, transcribing notes from a current case. He looked up when I stepped into his room and he spoke to me around a mouthful of Milky Way.

"I should have this wrapped up by the end of the day," O'Shannon said. He'd been working a fraud case for one of our corporate clients.

"Good," I said. "I may need you later. I just picked up a tail job that smells funny."

I showed him Bo's photo but it didn't set off any bells.

"Never seen the guy before," O'Shannon said.

"I'll ask around before I pick him up," I said.

Despite the heat, I pulled on my jacket and left the office.

My first and second stops were The Pink Flamingo, where I showed Bo's photo to Charlie Fischer, and a deli where I found Mannie Goldstein holding court in the back booth. Neither knew much about Bo, though Mannie provided his full name: Beauregard Delacroix. Mannie said, "He's up from Louisiana, fifteen, twenty years back."

My third stop was a boxer's gym on the near north side. I parked half a block away and watched the door. Marilyn had told me that Bo worked part-time at the gym and on Wednesdays he picked up his paycheck.

I left the car running, the air-conditioning cranked up to high, and watched the intermittent traffic in and out of the club. At a quarter to four, Bo arrived.

He was in and out of the club in less than five minutes, then he walked down the street away from me. I was out of the car and melting in the heat a moment later, walking quickly enough to match his pace, but not so fast as to attract attention.

I followed Bo to a check cashing service a block from the gym, then he crossed the street to a late model Lexus, keyed the lock, and slipped inside. He'd started the car and pulled away from the curb long before I could return to my

T-Bird.

I noted the license number of the Lexus on the back of one of my business cards. Then I returned to my car and cranked the air conditioning up before I used my new cell phone to call Sissy Ledbetter at the Department of Motor Vehicles. She'd been working there ever since she quit stripping and within five minutes I knew the name and address of the Lexus' registered owner.

It wasn't Bo.

I didn't recognize the name, so I phoned O'Shannon. I gave him Lily O'Connell's name and address.

"The name's familiar," he said. "I'll run it to ground, find out why."

After I disconnected from O'Shannon, I drove to the address on Marilyn's check.

I watched Marilyn's home from half a block away and soon Bo arrived. When Marilyn answered the door, Bo pulled her into his arms. She turned her face to the side and his kiss landed on the side of her head. She slipped her arms between them and pushed him away. They exchanged angry words. A moment later, Marilyn stepped into the house and slammed the front door behind her. Bo stormed to the Lexus, brought it to life, and made its tires smoke as he sped away.

It wasn't hard to follow Bo. I started my T-Bird, waited until Bo drove past, then pulled onto the street behind him.

My cell phone chirped. When I answered, O'Shannon said, "Lily O'Connell's a lawyer, handles divorce cases mostly, but she started practice as a defense attorney."

While I followed Bo across town, I punched Marilyn's home number into the cell phone and waited through nearly a dozen rings before she answered.

"I've had enough!" she shouted into the phone when she answered. "I told you I won't pay anything!"

"This is Nate Rose," I said, then listened as she choked

back whatever she had planned to say.

"What did you and Bo just fight about?" I asked.

As Marilyn answered, her voice regained the sultry smoothness I'd first heard in my office. "I'm ending it between us, Mr. Rose," she said. "He doesn't understand that."

By the time our conversation ended, Bo had pulled the Lexus to a halt in front of an upscale condo, and I'd found a parking spot nearby. The address matched the one Sissy Ledbetter had given me for the owner of the Lexus.

When Bo didn't come right out, I knew I wouldn't be satisfied waiting in the car. I climbed out, walked to the rear of the building, then pushed my way through a hedge and found a spot where I could see into the condo through the sliding glass door of the master bedroom.

The bedroom door inside was open and I could see down the hall to the living room. Bo stood with his back to the hall, speaking to a large-breasted blonde with closely-cropped hair and animated hands.

Bo stepped back as she jabbed a finger at him. The next time she jabbed a finger at him, Bo caught her wrist and twisted her arm to the side. She didn't flinch or wince. Instead, she slapped him with her free hand.

Bo bent low, drove his shoulder into her abdomen and stood, lifting her onto his shoulder. He turned and carried her down the hall toward the master bedroom and toward me.

I backed up, trying to squeeze into the bit of shadow in which I'd been hiding. I didn't need to bother since Bo and the blonde only had eyes for each other.

Bo dumped the blonde on the bed, then reached down and grabbed her blouse, tearing it off. Buttons popped and I heard at least one of them tick against the glass door.

The blonde scrambled to her feet.

Then she tore at his clothes with equal abandon, tugging at his belt and his zipper, dropping his pants to the floor.

When they finished stripping each other, Bo spun the blonde around, pressing her against the sliding glass door. Bo took her from behind, the door rattling with repeated pounding.

I watched their breath fog the glass until Bo finally finished and stepped away. The blonde peeled herself off the door a moment later. Then Bo disappeared through a doorway and she followed him.

I didn't wait for their return. I squeezed through the hedge and walked back to my car. Once in the car, I used my cell phone to dial the office.

"You have the Bar Association directory handy?" I asked as soon as Agnes answered.

"Right here."

"Tell me what Lily O'Connell looks like."

"Blonde, forties, stocky maybe," Agnes said a moment later. "It's a head-and-shoulders shot, so she might just be wearing padded shoulders."

I'd heard enough. Marilyn's boyfriend was doing the divorce lawyer on the side.

"Ah, shit," I said under my breath when I saw Bo stepping out of the lawyer's condo. I fumbled my keys out of my pocket and started the car. As the engine caught and I shifted the T-Bird into gear, I finished my conversation with Agnes and dropped the cell phone onto the seat beside me.

Bo settled into the Lexus and a moment later he backed the car out of its parking space. I followed him to what I presumed was his place, a second-floor walk-up not far from the gym where he worked.

I waited about two hours, then O'Shannon arrived to take over surveillance and I drove back to my apartment for a short night's sleep.

arrived at the office early to find Agnes already at her

desk, her fingers flying across her computer keyboard. She stopped to hand me three sheets of paper.

"I made a few calls this morning," she said. "Lily O'Connell once handled a misdemeanor assault for Bo Delacroix."

The details were in the papers Agnes handed me and I studied them at my desk. Bo had flattened a man's nose during a brawl at a south side bar and O'Connell had gotten him off with a small fine and time served.

From the office, I drove to Marilyn Richards' house and she escorted me into the living room. She sat at the end of the couch and I sat in an uncomfortable chair positioned at a right angle to the couch.

"It's been less that 24 hours. Do you have something for me already, Mr. Rose?" she asked.

"Nate," I said. "My friends call me Nate."

She reached out and touched my knee, her slim fingers warm through the thin material of my slacks. "I'd like to be your friend, Nate."

"Nothing to report, yet," I said. "But I have a few questions. The answers could help me."

She drew back her hand. "Go ahead, then."

"How did you meet Bo?"

"A . . . friend introduced us. She said he would take my mind off the divorce."

"Did he?"

"He's a very . . . athletic individual. Unbelievable stamina."

I looked a question at her.

"The last few years with Winston were . . . unsatisfying. We slept in separate bedrooms. I needed to rediscover that side of myself," she said. "Bo was the right man for that."

"But he isn't now?"

"He's ambitious, Nate." She touched my knee again and looked deep into my eyes. "I have a lot of money, and I need a man who'll love me for who I am, not for my bank balance."

O'Shannon and I alternated surveillance on Bo for the next three days. He spent one of those days at the gym and two evenings at the homes of recently divorced socialites.

The third night, I followed him home and waited until the lights in his apartment had been extinguished. Then I made my way up the stairs to Bo's apartment, picked the lock, and slipped inside. Neon light from the bar across the street filtered into the living room through the half-open curtains, enough so that I made my way to the bedroom without stumbling. The heatwave had broken early in the day and a cool breeze flowed through an open window on the far side of the room.

I pulled out my .45 and grasped it in my right fist. Then I kicked the end of Bo's bed. He sat straight up.

"Who the fuck are you?"

"A guy with a gun," I said.

"So what do you want?"

"You're a popular guy, Bo," I said. "A real ladies man."

"I get my share." He was sizing me up.

"Some might say you get more than your share," I continued. "You're doing some high class pussy these days. Maybe a little too upscale for the likes of you."

"What're you, somebody's ex?" Bo asked. "Jealous 'cause I'm heatin' the old lady's muffin?"

"How do you meet them, Bo? You aren't the country club type."

"I got a friend introduces me."

"A lawyer?"

"That's her," Bo said. "Lily's got lots of friends need a little attention. And they're all willin' to pay for it."

I let Bo continue without interruption.

"'Course, the photographer gets a piece of it," Bo said.

"A month, two months, maybe three is all most of them women can handle," he said. "After that I don't show up so often, but my lawyer friend shows these women a few photographs and suddenly they all need her on a monthly retainer."

I had my answer. I backed out of Bo's bedroom, then slipped out of his apartment and down the steps. He didn't follow.

I returned to the office, arriving only a few minutes before O'Shannon. We shared a few fingers of bourbon from a nearly empty bottle he pulled from his bottom desk drawer. His office had once belonged to my first partner, then had been a storage room for many years. O'Shannon had straightened the room up and, except for a trashcan overflowing with candy wrappers, he'd made it nearly as nice as mine.

As we drank, I told O'Shannon everything I'd learned, and he filled in a few missing details from his investigation. Marilyn Richards and both of the other socialites we'd seen Bo serving had had their divorces handled by Lily O'Connell.

By the time we'd emptied the bourbon, O'Shannon and I knew what we had to do. I drove home, slept most of the morning, then showered, shaved, and returned to the office to strategize with O'Shannon.

That night I picked the locks at Lily O'Connell's office and spent two hours going through her files. I left the building with an arm-load of file folders, photos, and negatives that none of her clients ever wanted to have see the light of day. I spent the next few hours in my office, sorting through everything.

I spent a lot of time staring at the photos, their explicitness distracting me from my primary objective. Over the course of nearly five years, Bo had been photographed with eighteen of Lily O'Connell's clients, including Marilyn Richards. The women were mostly in their thirties, though one was clearly pushing fifty and a pair of them barely looked old enough to be college graduates.

I don't know what any of them saw in Bo, but he certainly wasn't anything like the milque-toast husbands they'd given up. According to the files, none of the women would ever be strapped for cash, but all had some level of social prominence within the community. Not one could afford a scandal.

And that's where O'Connell took advantage of the women. According to the files, the lawyer received more than a million dollars a year in "retainer" fees from the 18 women, nearly as much as she earned handling divorce cases and other domestic litigation.

It was a sweet scam.

O'Shannon arrived at half past midnight. "Everything's set," he said. "I'll phone Skinny Reeves as soon as we know the address."

O'Shannon and I visited Bo's apartment and, after introducing his face to the plaster wall more times then either of us could count, he finally gave up the photographer's name. We convinced Bo to leave town that night and, by coincidence, the photographer's studio was destroyed in a fire that insurance investigators later determined was caused by faulty wiring.

Back at the office the next morning, I prepared eighteen separate envelopes and took seventeen of them to a courier service I trusted. By mid-afternoon, seventeen of Lily's clients would have the photographs and negatives of their trysts with Bo. By the end of the day, Lily O'Connell's client list would be severely truncated.

Then I phoned my client and arranged to meet at her home early that evening.

I laid a manila envelope on the coffee table in front of Marilyn.

"What's this?" She reached forward to pick up the envelope, opened it, and examined its contents. Then she looked at me. "You've seen these, I presume."

I nodded. "Some pretty rough stuff in there."

"It's what I thought I wanted," she said. "It's what I needed."

"Everything's there," I said. "Prints, negatives, everything."

"What do you want for this?"

"Day rate plus expenses," I said. "I'll have Agnes bill you for whatever the retainer didn't cover."

She stared at me for a moment. Then she wet her lips with the tip of her tongue and asked, "You're not interested in my money, are you, Nate?"

Even though the heatwave had ended earlier that week, I suddenly felt the temperature rise in Marilyn's living room. She was the type of woman I could fall for—the type of woman I had fallen for many times in the past—and I took a deep breath.

This time, I told myself, it was only business.

About the Author

Michael Bracken is the author of *Deadly Campaign, Even Roses Bleed, In the Town of Memories Dying and Dreams Unborn, Just in Time for Love, Psi Cops,* and nearly 700 shorter works published in Australia, Canada, China, England, Ireland, and the United States. He was born in Canton, Ohio, has traveled extensively throughout the U.S., and currently resides in Waco, Texas, with his wife, Sharon, and son, Ian. He has three other children — Ryan, Courtney, and Nigel — from a previous marriage.

Printed in the United States
6699